"You're one of the good guys, aren't you, Jack?"

Heat kindled in his eyes. "I don't know about that, but I think I should give you fair warning. You don't want to say things like that—or look at me like you're doing right now—unless you mean it."

She hesitated, realizing suddenly that they were getting close to the point where they had to choose to either keep things professional, or go over the line to personal. And once they crossed the line, they could decide not to go any further, but there was no going back. "You're nothing like I thought you were going to be."

"What were you expecting?"

"Someone who thinks being a cop gives him enough karma points to make up for him being pushy—or worse, indifferent—in other areas of his life." She broke off and blew out a breath. "Sorry."

"Don't be. It explains a few things."

Maybe so, but it didn't do anything to stop them from acting on the too-powerful attraction that would surely leave them breathless—and ultimately heartbroken.

JESSICA ANDERSEN

BEAR CLAW BODYGUARD

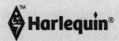

TORONTO NEW YORK LONDON
AMSTERDAM PARIS SYDNEY HAMBURG
STOCKHOLM ATHENS TOKYO MILAN MADRID
PRAGUE WARSAW BUDAPEST AUCKLAND

To the readers who have put Bear Claw State Park on the map.
Thank you!

Recycling programs
for this product may
not exist in your area.

ISBN-13: 978-0-373-69589-8

BEAR CLAW BODYGUARD

ABOUT THE AUTHOR

Jessica Andersen has worked as a geneticist, scientific editor, animal trainer and landscaper...but she's happiest when she's combining all of her many interests into writing romantic adventures that always have a twist of the unusual to them. Born and raised in the Boston area (Go, Sox!), Jessica can usually be found somewhere in New England, hard at work on her next happily-ever-after. For more on Jessica and her books, please check out www.JessicaAndersen.com and www.JessicaAndersenIntrigues.com.

Books by Jessica Andersen

CAST OF CHARACTERS

Detective Jack Williams—While a deadly drug is taking a personal toll on the streets, this dedicated Bear Claw cop with heartbreak in his past has no interest in babysitting a cute visiting scientist with a Napoleon complex.

Dr. Tori Bay—Tori might be one of the top plant-disease specialists in the US National Parks Service, but she's never before seen anything like the disease in Bear Claw's Forgotten Forest…or been paired with a local like Jack. When it becomes clear that someone doesn't want them near the hot zone, she must rely on Jack for 24/7 protection.

Chondra—Tori's friend and head lab tech is willing to help her out on the sly when their bosses shut down the increasingly dangerous investigation into the Bear Claw outbreak.

Percy Proudfoot—Bear Claw's mayor is a notorious penny-pincher…but is there something far more devious going on?

The Shadow Militia—The armed men and their military trucks disappeared into the forest months ago…but are they really gone? And what do they want?

Detective Tucker McDermott—Jack's boss and good friend is being run ragged trying to get the deadly drugs off the city streets on one hand, while trying to protect the vast state park system on the other.

The Investor—The mastermind behind it all is a shadowy figure at best. Will the Bear Claw P.D. be able to bring his identity to light in time?

Chapter One

"You're off the case, Jack—period, end of discussion."

The decision being handed down by Tucker McDermott—who was the head of the Bear Claw P.D.'s Homicide Division and, therefore, Jack's immediate superior—wasn't a shocker, but that didn't stop the veteran detective from wanting to launch himself from the visitor's chair in Tucker's office and pace. Or maybe go over the desk to try and shake some sense into his boss. But that kind of behavior was what had gotten him into this mess in the first place, so Jack made himself take a breath and do a three-count before saying, "You know you can't afford to bench me right—"

"What part of 'end of discussion' are you not getting?"

Tucker's don't-mess-with-me tone probably should have been a clue, but it wasn't until Jack saw a muscle twitch at the corner of his friend's jaw that he got it. "Oh." He leaned back. "Damn. This is coming from Mendoza, isn't it?"

"Even if the chief hadn't made the call, I probably would have pulled you off the case."

"I… Yeah." Frustration welled up, and it wasn't entirely aimed at Tucker. It'd been an accident, but the reality was that Jack had had his hands on the witness when he went down. And with Mayor Proudfoot slashing the city's budgets like he was clear-cutting for a financial strip mine, the P.D. couldn't afford the bad press.

"And you did it in front of a rook," Tucker said, reaching for the antacids that'd taken up residence in his top drawer over the past month, ever since the birth of his daughter had coincided with the explosion of two major cases that had, thanks to budget cuts, landed in his lap.

"Doran won't get the wrong message," Jack said of his rookie partner. "He's solid."

"Maybe, but you're not. Ever since this case got hot, you've been on the warpath."

At six foot and one-ninety, with prematurely salted chestnut hair and light blue eyes, Jack didn't make any claim to native blood. But, yeah, he had some warpath going on these days. What Bear Claw cop didn't? Out in the Colorado wilderness they were playing hide-and-seek with members of a militia so slippery they were practically ghosts, while in the city they were losing the battle against a new fad drug that was ripping through the underground and leaving bodies behind.

Leaning in, Jack grated, "You need me out there on the streets. We're way too far behind the curve on this Death Stare thing."

That was what the media was calling the new drug, thanks to the fixed, almost terrified looks on the victims' faces. Why the hell that plus the number of bodies piling up hadn't been enough to scare people off, he would never understand. But to the hard-core users, the promise of an incredible high was apparently worth the risk.

Tucker shook his head. "You screwed up, Jack. You know it, I know it, Mendoza knows it…and even if the higher-ups weren't involved, I can't ignore the fact that you're way too invested in this case, and it's making you unreliable." His eyes softened a bit, showing the tired guy, new father and dedicated cop behind the thick "I'm the boss" layer. "Look, I'm sorry, but if I let you back on the case now Mendoza will have my butt in a sling faster than you can say 'what the hell is this damn drug, and where is it coming from?'"

Unfortunately, there was no arguing that one. Jack shifted in his chair, still not letting himself pace off the restless frustration even though he was tempted. "So put me on background stuff. Hell, I'll even ride a desk if that's what you want. But don't boot me all the way off the investigation. I need to—" He broke off. "Look, I need to be in on this."

"You should've thought of that before you put your hands on your wit. Accident or not, I can't let it go."

"I… Damn it." Jack slouched back in his chair and scrubbed a hand over his face, knowing that Tucker was right, he had only himself—along with a grease spot and volatile city politics—to blame. "This sucks."

"No argument there." Tucker slid a single-page printout across his desk. "Take this. It's your new assignment."

Jack eyeballed it, found airline info for an incoming flight landing at the local hub mid-morning and heaved a sigh. "You want me to play taxi? Who for?"

Actually, that wasn't the worst gig he could've gotten handed. There had been numerous law enforcement comings and goings in the past few weeks, and Tucker had pressed senior cops into chauffeur duty a few times before to get some informal lines of communication open between the local and federal teams.

"You're meeting a Dr. Tori Bay…and you're going to be

doing more than playing taxi. You'll be escorting her out to the Forgotten and watching her back while she's there."

Jack's tension eased some. If he couldn't be on the drug investigation, this case was the next best thing. A few weeks earlier, the members of the Shadow Militia—also a name that came courtesy of the media—had attacked a ranger, torched large sections of the state forest, shot down a government helicopter, nearly killed two deputized cops...and then vanished from the camo-netted campsite that had been hidden within the Forgotten, a barren region at the farthest edge of the state park.

It wasn't just the three dozen or so people who had been living at the campsite who had vanished, either; there hadn't been any sign of the equipment and heavy vehicles that had left tracks in the drought-parched dirt. With the feds unable to pick up anything on satellite imagery or closer-in scans, the investigation had fallen back on forensics and old-school tracking. And even those avenues had come up dry, as if the entire armed camp had simply disappeared into thin air.

Given the city's issues a couple of years ago with terrorist mastermind al-Jihad, the feds were taking the threat seriously, sending their best and coordinating things with the Bear Claw P.D. So Jack made a "bring it on" gesture. "The militia case? Hell, yeah, sign me up."

But Tucker shook his head. "This isn't about the militia. It's about the trees."

"The..." Jack trailed off, remembering the weird tree fungus that'd also been found in that same part of the Forgotten, along with a remnant population of barred eagles, which had previously been thought extinct. Thanks to those discoveries, there had also been a steady stream of scientists coming and going from the barren, dangerous wasteland. His stomach sank. "You can't possibly want me to babysit a tree hugger. That's a ranger's job, or maybe a rook's." The Bear Claw Canyon Park Service had been coordinating with the P.D. to keep the scientists safe, both from the militants who might or might not still be in the area and from the inherent dangers of the backcountry.

"For the next couple of days it's your job," Tucker retorted. "Be grateful I'm not suspending you."

"Right," Jack said, trying to get the bitterness and "oh, hell, no" out of his voice. "Punishment."

Granted, he deserved a smack-down for his behavior, but it seriously sucked that his reassignment was going to hurt the ongoing investigations. The department was already so shorthanded that the detectives were partnering up with uniforms; his being out in the Forgotten on babysitting duty sure as hell wasn't going to help.

"I'd prefer to call it a few days out in the woods to get your head put back on straight."

"I can pull it together. You don't need to send me off to the Forgotten."

But Tucker shook his head even as he said, "Yeah, I really do. It wasn't just Mendoza leaning on me; it was the mayor's office, too. I need you off their radar screens for the next few days at an absolute minimum, until something else comes along to take their minds off your blowing one of the few leads we've had since the overdoses started."

Jack grimaced, huffing out a breath as he came to grips with the no-win he was up against—and the fact that it was purely his fault that he was up against it. "Okay, fine. I'll do it." Like there had ever been any real question on the matter. He hesitated, seeing the strain in Tucker's face and knowing the other man had undoubtedly gone to bat against the higher-ups on his behalf. "And thanks. I know it could've been a whole lot worse."

"Yeah, so behave yourself." Tucker leaned back in his chair. "And keep your eyes open, okay? The abandoned campsite is smack in the middle of the worst of the tree fungus."

Jack narrowed his eyes at that little tidbit, which said there was more to this assignment than babysitting and navel gazing. "You think there's a connection between the tree crud and the militia?"

"Maybe, maybe not…and even so, what's the chicken and what's the egg? The environmental chemists didn't find any evidence of weird contamination, but there are stranger things on heaven and earth, and all that. Maybe this Dr. Bay will see something the others missed…or maybe you will."

Jack took what felt like the first real breath he'd drawn since he heard the brittle crack of his witness's wrist. It wasn't the Death Stare case, but at least he was still on active duty, and with an unofficial sanction to work the militia case. More, if he stayed out of trouble long enough he was pretty sure Tucker would shift him back over to the Death Stare investigation, which was where he wanted— needed—to be.

The key there being "stay out of trouble," he reminded himself as he rose and grabbed the airline info. "Guess I should go get my tree doctor. Any idea what she looks like?"

"No clue." One corner of Tucker's mouth lifted. "Maybe

she'll turn out to be a tall, cool blonde. That's your type, right?"

"Used to be," Jack said, and shot Tucker a kiss-my-butt grin. "Too bad you got to Alyssa before I did."

That was total bull. There'd never been anything between Jack and Alyssa Locke-turned-McDermott, the CSI who had become Tucker's wife, but as a diversion it worked just fine, especially given that Alyssa had the long, cool blonde thing going on in spades.

Tucker just grinned. "Eat your heart out, bachelor boy." He tapped the clamshell photo frame on his desk. "I've got myself two long cool blondes of my very own." Technically, only Alyssa fit the bill; two-month-old baby Laurel was more along the lines of short and wide-eyed, though the fine wisps of hair caught in a bubble gum–pink bow were definitely blond. But the two of them together, yeah, that brought a pang. It was what Jack had thought he'd had lined up, the future he'd seen himself living.

Hadn't worked out, though, and he'd moved on. Maybe he hadn't found his one and only yet, but he'd worked out his process—slow and steady won the race when it came to relationships, at least as far as he was concerned—and he'd come to grips with being single long after most everyone else in his generation of Williamses had paired off.

In the meantime, though, he had a good job, good friends and Bear Claw was home, even if it was having its problems these days.

It was those problems that occupied the forefront of his mind as he strode across the parking lot to his SUV, subverting the more pleasant thoughts of a tall, cool anything. And as he started mentally reviewing what he knew of the Forgotten and the militia case, he decided it wouldn't hurt to call a few contacts on the way out to the airport and make sure he was up to speed.

He might not want this assignment, but it was his ticket back on to the more important investigation. Besides, he'd be damned if anything happened to a visiting scientist on his watch.

Chapter Two

Tori saw the guy the moment she hit the baggage claim area, and only partly because the badge on his belt marked him as her Bear Claw P.D. liaison.

Mostly it was because he was really hard to miss.

In fact, she was pretty sure the brief hesitation in the determined stride of her seatmate from the plane came from a "Hello, handsome" moment rather than dismay over the "Delayed" sign blinking next to their flight number on the board.

Tori and the tall, blonde businesswoman might have waged a low-grade and unstated war over foot room and control of their supposedly shared armrest during the endless-feeling flight, but in that moment she had a feeling they were united in feminine appreciation.

The guy was maybe a shade over six feet, with dark auburn hair, piercing, pale blue eyes and an aggressive jut of a nose that made him seriously good scenery in a full-on masculine sort of way. He sported a hint of silver at his temples, but Tori put him at closer to thirty than forty, rugged and handsome in a way that made her think of mountains and fast-running rivers.

Wearing jeans, a light blue button-down that was open at the throat and rolled up over his tanned forearms and a pair of hiking boots with enough scars to suggest they had seen some rough trails, he probably should've looked like he had just stepped out of an ad for an expensive cologne, but even without the badge, she would've pegged him as a cop. It was in the way he held himself, the way he watched the flow of human traffic.

Or, rather, the way he *had* been watching the flow. Now he was watching the blonde.

Typical, Tori thought on a beat of disgust, and didn't let herself try to match the other woman's long-legged stride as she swaggered over to the cop, who was lounging against a support beam, looking like someone had dropped a piece of the wilderness in among the overprocessed, touristy posters that lined the walls.

If Blondie hadn't spent the entire flight being a space invader, Tori might have admired the way she moved past her prey, pretending to ignore him as she frowned prettily up at the display. As it was, she sneered inwardly as the cop took the bait and said something to her. Tori wasn't close enough to catch his opening line, but as she drew near, Blondie glanced at him, her expression caught between interest and triumph as she purred, "Are you looking for someone?"

He nodded. "Yes, indeed. And I believe I've found her." He looked over and down—*way* down—to Tori. "Dr. Bay, I presume?"

Blondie's smile instantly lost its wattage and her face took on a look of *Really?* But Tori barely noticed because she was busy doing a double take of her own, as surprise that he had noticed her was compounded by the *hoo-boy* of having those baby blues locked on to her.

His outdoorsy vibe might've made her think of the

mountains, but his eyes were the cerulean of a perfectly flat high-country lake beneath a cloudless sky. The kind of lake that hikers would take a day's climb to reach, and then be grateful to simply sit and stare. Which was exactly what she was doing.

Staring up at him. Like a five-foot-nothing dork.

Say something, idiot!

"Yes, I'm Dr. Bay," she blurted, loud enough to make herself wince. Forcing her voice to something approaching its normal businesslike tone, she added, "How did you recognize me?"

The university typically didn't send much advance info on their field researchers, never mind photos. Then again, the people requesting her services typically didn't insist on police protection either.

The corners of his eyes crinkled arrestingly. "Given the knapsack, hiking boots and the insignia on your windbreaker, I figured it was a good bet you were the tree doctor."

Catching Blondie's smirk in her peripheral vision, Tori bristled. She didn't need to look down at herself to know that she was rocking the earthy-crunchy factor in jeans and a plain forest-green T-shirt, along with a U.S. Plant Pathology Association windbreaker that was a couple of sizes too big because they didn't come in extra small. And, yeah, given that she had her bark-brown hair pulled back in a stubby ponytail and was wearing her glasses because airplanes did wonky things to her contacts, she wasn't even close to being in Blondie's league. And not just because she was lacking the designer suit, stilettos and a foot of height.

Worse, she had actually bothered to catalog those differences.

Hello, she thought loudly, hoping both her libido and her brain would listen up, *you're not here for a fieldwork fling. You're here to do a job.* Granted, she'd combined the two more than once in the past, but this particular job fell under the category of "potential disaster, probably shouldn't let yourself get distracted, hunky escort or not."

Besides, he was a cop.

Deliberately, she put her head back in the work zone where it belonged. The U.S. National Park Service was worried about the newly discovered breeding population of barred eagles, and the strange, threadlike fungus that was killing huge chunks of forest near the eagles' nesting area. Given the ecological chaos caused by the recent oak-blight epidemic in California's Point Reyes Park, the Park Service wasn't taking any chances in Bear Claw Canyon. When the local scientists hadn't been able to crack the fungus's life cycle or the real cause of the problems the trees were experiencing, Tori had gotten the call.

Her family might not understand her choosing to save trees rather than people, but she was very good at what she did.

Giving the cop a cool look, she said, "I prefer the term 'phytopathologist.' Or 'plant disease epidemiologist' is okay, too."

He raised an eyebrow. "How about we go with Tori and Jack instead? Seems easier, and half the time when I hear 'Detective Williams,' I turn around to see if my dad or uncle are standing behind me."

Which meant he wasn't just a cop, he was straight out of a cop family, with all the "save the world and pat the little lady on the head" machismo that it entailed. Or maybe that was just *her* family, she thought, trying to smooth out the sudden tug of irritation he hadn't earned.

Which just left her realizing that she had just told her local liaison to use her professional titles. God, she was still such a dweeb sometimes, especially when faced with a guy who felt just that little bit out of her league, turning him into a challenge.

Making herself grin rather than groan, she nodded. "Tori and Jack it is."

She didn't bother asking herself what it was about this guy that had her caught somewhere between lust and dorksville. He was seriously hot; she was exhausted by having done a week's worth of grant writing in two days to make this trip; and it had been a few months since she and her last equally on-the-go lover, Greene, had called it quits. So she was noticing the handsome detective in a chemically combustible way, and it was making her a little silly. Okay, more than a little.

Focus. "We should get going. I understand that the site is pretty far off the beaten path."

"That's an understatement. We'll be using Ranger Station Fourteen as a base camp and driving out to the Forgotten from there on a daily basis."

"Wait. What?" She frowned up at him. Way up, which made her feel short, and in turn, irritated her. "We won't need the ranger station. We're camping out at the site for the duration." That was SOP for the more remote locations, and she'd been assured there would be no problem.

His expression tightened and those lake waters chilled. "Not with an armed militia out there, we're not."

"An…" She blew out a breath, not liking the sound of

that one bit. "I was under the impression that the area was secure."

"That might be the official line, but it's not the reality as far as my contacts within the investigation are concerned. So here's the deal: either we bunk at Ranger Station Fourteen and day-trip it out to the Forgotten, or you hold off on your investigation until we've got a real handle on the Shadow Militia. Your call."

Even as jitters took up residence in her stomach, she narrowed her eyes at him, trying to figure out if he was on the level or if this was another version of the familiar song that went *I've got better things to do than drag you around; I wish you'd go away.*

Most of the time, her escorts were happy to bring her to the infected site and eager to hear what she had to say about their problem. Occasionally, though, she ran into the other kind: the ones who didn't want her around, whether because she'd been foisted on them, they saw her as a threat or because they didn't want to be anyone's chaperone. She didn't peg this guy as foistable or threatened, but he also didn't strike her as the type to volunteer to babysit a visiting scientist. What she didn't know was whether he was overemphasizing the danger in an effort to run her off…or if there was really a chance that there were still armed killers hiding somewhere in the Forgotten, which had the rep of being seriously rough territory in its own right.

Her jitters edged toward nerves, but she held her ground because logic said it couldn't be that bad or her assignment would've been called off. Whether or not she agreed with it—which she didn't—investigations into plant outbreaks often got shunted back behind human factors, and she'd had cases canceled over far smaller problems before.

Testing the waters, she said, "If it's that dangerous, I'm surprised your bosses okayed the investigation." Glancing down, she went for her phone. "Maybe I should call—"

He caught her wrist. "Don't."

For a few agonizing seconds all she could feel was the warm touch of his hand and the press of his fingers over her pulse. Heat washed up her throat to her face, bringing a heady mix of attraction and nerves. Her heart pounded, she couldn't catch her breath, and… *Knock it off,* she told herself. *He's not that hot.*

Okay, maybe he was, but that didn't change his basic makeup: namely, a cop from a cop family. What was more, she had her answer. He was trying to play her.

Tugging her arm from his grip, she regarded him coolly. "Level with me, then. How high is the risk really, Detective?"

"Too high." But when she just kept looking at him, he glanced away and made an annoyed sound. "Look, it's nothing solid at this point, or else you're right, your people or mine would've already called things off. But some of the cops on the task force—good cops, people I trust— say their guts are telling them that the militia is still in the area. There've been some signs." He looked back at her, his eyes making her think once more of clear, still lakes and reflected skies. But there was zero sunshine in his voice when he continued, "If I'm under orders to keep you safe, then I wouldn't be doing my job if I didn't suggest that you hold off on your investigation until we're sure the area is secure. The Forgotten has been there for a long time—another few weeks or months won't make a difference to the trees."

It wasn't what he said that had annoyance bubbling up inside her; it was the way he said it, with practically a verbal pat on the head. *Stop being so dramatic, the woods will be fine. And even if they're not, who cares? There are lots of trees in the forest—ha ha.*

And wasn't that just typical? she thought as anger flared to replace the heat of his touch. "For your information, Detective, we're not just talking about trees here. This could be the beginning of a widespread ecological collapse that could take out the native wildlife in the area...including the last remaining wild population of barred eagles that we know of. Not to mention that weeks or months absolutely *could* make a difference when it comes to a fast-moving infection and the disruption it can cause to a fragile ecosystem. In fact, *days* could make a difference, which is why I canceled a speaking engagement and fast-tracked a grant application to get my butt down here as soon as I found out about the problem in the Forgotten." She paused, though, because there were still some solid nerves beneath the irritation. And although she might be tripping over her tongue right now with her handsome escort, she wasn't an idiot. "Please, Detective, tell me honestly—and we're talking the absolute truth here, taking your other cases or whatever else is going on inside your head out of the mix—how much real and concrete danger will I be in if we go out there?"

His gaze sharpened on her with surprise and, she thought, maybe a bit of respect. *Didn't expect the pint-size plant nerd to push back, did you?*

He was paying attention now, though, with none of the

earlier eye crinkle that said he was humoring her. And his voice was dead serious when he said, "Okay, Doc, here's the deal. There's no hard evidence that the militants are still in the area, and there hasn't been any sign of daytime movement, at least not that the surveillance has managed to pick up. It's just gut feelings and suspicions right now. So, no, there's no hard evidence. And if you're certain that you want to do this, we'll go. But I'm going to drive you in and out each day from Station Fourteen, and camping out up at the site just isn't an option. Take it or leave it." He paused, then said almost grudgingly, "For what it's worth, I know the situation's not perfect, and I'm sorry that it's going to complicate your investigation."

He even looked like he meant it, which had her tension easing somewhat, and her shoulders coming down a bit from their tight "trying to be taller" squareness. "Okay," she conceded. "The commute is going to slow me down, but I'll work around it somehow."

"And you'll do what I tell you once we reach the Forgotten?"

"I won't do anything stupid."

"That's not what I asked."

No, it wasn't, but she knew better than to make blanket promises like that. Re-squaring her shoulders and not letting herself get trapped in those eyes, which made her want to agree to just about anything, she said, "If we're talking about cop stuff, then yes, of course you're in charge. But when it comes to fieldwork, I'm going to be calling the shots on when, where and what. And the 'when' is now and the 'where' is out at the infection site. I know you probably think what I do is lightweight compared to your job, but if my suspicions are correct, Bear

Claw Canyon could be looking at a major ecosystem collapse unless we can—or, rather, unless *I* can—contain the spread of this disease."

As if to punctuate her words, the luggage carousel finally rumbled to life, the "Delayed" sign blinked off, and her flight number came up in glowing pixels. The luggage started spitting out almost immediately, and Blondie grabbed a couple of Vuittons and clicked away with only a single last look over her shoulder, which the detective didn't acknowledge. He kept his eyes locked on Tori, and she stared right back.

Finally, he sighed, nodded and broke their eyeball stalemate. "Okay, we'll head out to the station and go from there. Which bags are yours?"

"I've got them." As her two bulging duffels trundled their way around the conveyer, she stepped forward and snagged them. She was aware of his gaze following her as she handled the heavy load with a combination of leverage and a bone-deep refusal to let him see her wobble. When she turned back to him, he was holding out a hand. She eyed it, trying not to notice the faint but capable calluses or how much bigger it was than her own. "You want to shake on it?"

"We could do that. Or you could give me those bags and we can hit the road."

She wasn't entirely sure if they had reached an agreement, a standoff or what. But as she handed over one of the duffels and stubbornly kept the other for herself, and then followed him out to a capable-looking dark green SUV, she knew for darned sure that she was going to need to be on her toes around this guy if she planned on running the investigation on her terms. After all, high-country lakes might appear to be a simple, beautiful blue on the surface, but they often had submerged dangers that could snag the unwary boater…especially if she was too busy being caught up in the scenery to see the danger before she went overboard.

Chapter Three

By the time he steered his SUV onto the final section of road leading up to Ranger Station Fourteen, Jack was more than ready to get the hell out of the car. He was riled up, wound tight and needed to move so badly that it was taking him an almost physical effort to not stomp on the gas and blast up the last few miles going way too fast for safety.

It wasn't because of anything his passenger had done either. Before they even reached the highway, Tori had pulled off her windbreaker, wadded it up against the door-frame to use as a pillow and fallen instantly asleep. Nope, she wasn't the problem at all; *he* was. Because with her sleeping so soundly, he was free to glance over at her time and again, trying to figure her out.

When she had first come through the security check-point, he'd instantly gotten the impression of movement and energy, creating a vitality that had filled the space around her so thoroughly that he hadn't realized how tiny she was until she was right there in front of him. Even then, she had radiated such competence in her practical clothes and tomboy appearance—a cute tomboy in glasses and a ponytail, but a tomboy nonetheless—that he had told himself she'd be okay in the Forgotten.

Heck, she'd had no problem standing up to him, had she? She'd gone right after him with a one-two punch of logic and determination, with the subtle threat of "let's call our bosses" behind it all, much as Tucker's wife, Alyssa, might have done, or any one of the other rock star lady cops Bear Claw was fortunate enough to have in the field.

He hadn't anticipated that sort of grit, guts and determination from a tree doctor—he'd been expecting someone quieter and a lot less fiery, he supposed, and that was probably what he got for making assumptions.

Now, though, seeing her asleep with one hand folded beneath her head, the other curled loosely around the seat belt where it crossed her chest, he was acutely aware that if he gripped her wrist his fingers would overlap his thumb almost fully. And, granted, that had nothing to do with her competence as a scientist…but it sure had him twitchy about bringing her out to the backcountry.

Lucky for me she's not the long, cool blonde Tucker was talking about, he thought. Because it was going to be bad enough dividing his attention between his diminutive protectee and the militia case; the last thing he needed was to have any kind of inappropriate attraction rear its head. And, hello, why was he even thinking about that? She was here for a few days, a week or two at the most, which was nowhere near long enough to start something like that.

"We're here," he announced as the SUV rolled past the rustic, T-shaped building that housed Ranger Station Fourteen—empty now, with the season having closed a few weeks earlier—and continued on to the quirky little house beyond it: an old research observatory that head ranger Matt Blackthorn had converted into his private quarters, and where he lived more or less year-round despite the harsh conditions.

Matt was every inch an ex-cop even though he didn't like to talk about his time on a city force far away. The ranger didn't like to talk about much really, although that had been improving since he fell for Gigi Lynd, the pretty CSI who'd wound up embroiled in the initial round of attacks by the Shadow Militia. Last Jack had heard from Gigi—who had done some ride-alongs with him and become a casual friend—she and Matt were keeping a sharp eye on things up at Fourteen but hadn't seen any evidence of the militia. He hadn't been able to get hold of her today, though, and was looking forward to getting an update from her and Matt.

As he pulled into the parking area in front of the observatory and killed the engine, Tori sat up and blinked around, her brown eyes looking owlish behind her glasses, and then lighting as she took in their surroundings.

And, yeah, Matt's house was pretty cool, almost an inland lighthouse, with two levels of living space and a tall platform sprouting from one side. Towering high above the surrounding trees, it overlooked sweeping, rock-strewn vistas on all sides, some furred with a light, high-altitude tree covering, others bare. It was all drought-dry and dusty with ash from the wildfires that had leveled large portions of the forest to the south and west of Station Fourteen, but he still thought it was a seriously cool sight.

Her lips curved and she sighed. "Oh, this is wonderful."

Restless energy kicked through him like a jet on afterburners, making him want to… Hell, he didn't know what he wanted to do except get moving. Maybe Tucker was right about his needing some time and space to get his head clear after all.

Jerking a thumb toward the main door, he said, "Come on in. I need to pick up some extra gear before we head out to the site." A glance at the sky had him frowning. "If you even want to bother going up there today, that is. You're really going to get only a few hours out at the site before we have to call it a night."

Although there was a road between Fourteen and the Forgotten now, it was questionable at best, treacherous at worst, and there was no point in tackling it after dark.

"I'll take what I can get," she said firmly. "While you're loading your stuff, I'll change out of my airplane clothes and drop off some of my stuff if there's a place for it."

"There should be. It'll be tight quarters with you, me, Matt and Gigi, but we'll make it work."

Once he let himself through the unlocked front door, though, the first thing he saw was a note lying on the butcher-block breakfast bar, with his name scrawled at the top. A quick scan told him that things weren't going to be nearly as crowded as he had thought…and he really didn't want to analyze why that information had his gut fisting on a low burn of heat.

Clearing his throat, he said, "Matt and Gigi are going to be out of town for the next few days. Looks like we'll have the run of the place, along with a little extra elbow room."

She avoided his eyes and shrugged. "Fine by me either way. I'm used to living in close quarters, and most of the time we're here, I'll be working on the data and samples I've collected. Don't worry about entertaining me. The more I work, the faster you can get back to whatever you were doing before you got stuck babysitting me."

"I'm not… Hmm." He caught her faint grin, and almost wanted to laugh at himself, restlessness and all. "Hell. Go dump your stuff and we'll get moving."

She might be tiny, but she gave as good as she got.

Nodding, she strode across the lower level, which had the kitchen at one end, a good-size fireplace at the other, bracketing an open space filled with cushy couches and chairs strewn with colorful pillows and throws that were undoubtedly Gigi's influence. She headed for the spiral staircase off in the far corner, but as she reached it, she turned back. "Sorry, I'm on autopilot. I'm in the guest room upstairs, right?"

"Yeah. I'll be on the couch, keeping an eye on the perimeter." The main station house had recently been rebuilt after the militia members torched it as a diversionary tactic after all, and with the other rangers stationed on the ski slopes for the winter, they were going to be alone up there.

It wouldn't pay for him to let down his guard. On the contrary, it could be a huge mistake. And if, deep down inside, he knew damn well that his taking the couch also had more than a little to do with his having noticed that behind those glasses her brown eyes were lush and gorgeous, and framed by some of the longest lashes he'd ever seen, he was the only one who needed to have any inkling of it, or of the way his heart skidded a little at the thought that the two of them would be alone together tonight, on either end of a spiral staircase.

She looked at him for an extra moment, making him wonder what she saw, but then she nodded and headed upstairs.

He didn't watch her go, instead turning to the pile of gear Matt had left for him, which included additional fire-power and survival gear. He thought the water purifier was overkill—especially given that they were in the middle of a drought—but there was plenty of room in the SUV, so he figured he'd load it all on the "better safe than sorry" theory. And he had asked the ranger to hook him up with everything he thought they might need out at the Forgot-ten.

Ten minutes later, as he came back in for the third and last load, he saw Tori coming down the stairs. And he stopped dead, his brain vapor locking and his body going on red alert, and his only coherent thought one of *Oh, hell.*

He was in serious trouble.

She wasn't wearing her windbreaker or glasses any-more, and those changes made way too much of a differ-ence. Gone was the impression of an adolescent owl or a teenager wearing her boyfriend's jacket. In its place was the sight of a woman who might not be built big, but she was built right. Her legs were long in proportion to her body, and her slim waist accentuated with a webbed util-ity belt fitted through the loops of cargo pants that hugged her hips and moved lovingly with her as she came toward him. Her T-shirt was tight across a pair of surprisingly full breasts and snugged in at her waist and across a flat stomach that showed just a hint of a feminine curve.

She was carrying a knapsack over one shoulder, and the combined effect made him think of coeds and col-lege. Hesitating near the breakfast bar, she said, "What's wrong?"

In other words, he was staring. And that thing he'd been thinking about there not being a problem with attraction?

Yeah. That had just gone straight out the window. She might not be long, cool or blonde, but he was attracted all right.

Yanking his attention to the last of the gear he hadn't yet put in the truck, he set his jaw. "Nothing. Everything's just fine." He would make damn sure of it, in fact. Grabbing the last of the stuff, he turned away. "Come on, let's get moving."

As far as he was concerned, the sooner she finished her studies and headed back wherever she had come from, the better, because right now he couldn't afford the distraction. He had to protect her, look for clues on the militia and get back on the Death Stare case as quickly as possible. The victims might be nothing more than junkies to some, but as far as he was concerned, they were just as important as any other group of victims. Which meant that he didn't have time for big brown eyes or surprising breasts, or the way his body tightened as he heard her come outside behind him.

And even if he did have time, he reminded himself as he stowed the last of his gear, he wouldn't be spending it with another woman who was just passing through. Been there, done that, bought the tux.

By the time Jack parked the SUV in a small clump of scrubby, stunted trees that looked exactly like the last thousand such clumps they had passed since leaving Ranger Station Fourteen, Tori wasn't sure which was worse: the way he was grimly ignoring her, or the fact that it bothered her far more than it should.

Throughout the drive, one part of her had been cataloging the passing scenery, tapping notes into her hand-held and generally getting a feel for the northernmost reaches of the state park and the damage done by the recent drought conditions. Another part of her, though, had been all too aware of Jack as he navigated the rugged one-lane track with deceptive ease and one hand on the wheel. Beneath that layer of calm, though, there was an electric tension that was transmitted in his every shift and breath, and in the few glances he sent her way.

She didn't kid herself into thinking that he, too, was far too aware of the small space they were sharing. No, he was undoubtedly still seething over having to babysit a "tree doctor" instead of working other, more important—to him, at least—cases. But even that didn't seem to be enough to make her hormones cool their jets, because as he climbed out of the SUV and turned back to retrieve a shotgun from a box in the backseat, she caught herself admiring the smooth grace of his big body, and the lethal economy of his practiced movements, which made her feel simultaneously safer and more exposed.

More, as she set about pulling the nonessentials from her knapsack, lightening the load for her first look around the site, she was acutely conscious of the way he slung the shotgun across his back with an easy, practiced move that brought a shiver of pure feminine appreciation.

Still, though, while he might be easy on the eyes and practically oozing outdoorsy pheromones, facts were facts: he was a cop; he was a local; and, justified or not, he was making it difficult for her to do her job. *Three strikes and you're out.*

She should do herself a favor and remember that.

Focus. She needed to focus, darn it. Forcing herself not to watch him as he walked an ever-widening spiral away from the vehicle, scanning the territory as he went, she pinched the bridge of her nose and closed her eyes. When she did, the world spun slowly, warning her that she was more tired and jet-lagged than she'd even realized. Which explained her overactive libido but warned her that she needed to pay attention to her surroundings, not her escort. The Colorado backcountry could be seriously unforgiving, as could a mishandled investigation.

The scuff of a footstep had her straightening and turning to face him, hoping that he couldn't see anything in her face—not the fatigue, not the knowledge that she wasn't at her best and certainly not the buzz that entered her bloodstream as he drew close, eyes still scanning their surroundings, then going to the sky as he said, "You'll have about three hours before we need to turn back, and even at that time we're going to be getting in later than I like."

His voice sounded strange to her after so much quiet between them. He didn't offer an explanation or apology, but then again, he didn't owe her either of those things. Regardless of what her hormones thought, they were nothing more than temporary business acquaintances. And if he could keep it professional despite not wanting to be there, she could do the same despite wanting… Well, better not go there.

Dredging up a professional smile and keeping a tight rein on both her thought process and her tendency to blurt the first thing that came to mind, especially when she felt a little out of her depth, she nodded. "Like I said before, I'll take what I can get. Are we at the edge of the infected area?" The trees around them appeared normal, with none of the ghostly white filaments she'd seen in the photographs that had been sent to her by the prior Park Service investigator.

"Yeah. The white stuff starts about fifty feet from here and stretches all the way to the river, which is a few miles away. We can walk it or drive it, your call."

She didn't make the mistake of thinking the "your call" would extend one iota beyond when it suited him, but had to give him credit for trying. "It'll take me a couple of hours to take preliminary samples and measurements, so parking here and hiking works for me. Then tomorrow I'd like to start from the river and spiral in from there."

"Sounds like a plan."

It didn't take her long to select the gear she wanted to carry with her and load it into her knapsack, then jettison a few of the less crucial pieces so she wouldn't kill herself trying to carry it. Jack stood nearby the whole time, keeping watch. With the shotgun slung across his back and a 9 mm in a hip holster, and his eyes scanning the trees with practiced intensity, he didn't look like any cop she'd dealt with before. There was no badge or polyester, no subtle twitch that said he was more comfortable with civilization than out in the backcountry. Instead, there was the deep stillness she associated with hunters and spiritualists, though he didn't strike her as either of those things, or at least not entirely. He was...different, she decided. Unexpected.

And she really needed to stop trying to figure out her chaperone and do her darned job. "Ready?" she said too brightly.

He gave her a look that said they weren't headed off to a picnic and she didn't need to sound so happy about it, but aloud, he said only, "You take point and I'll watch our backs. You see anything suspicious, yell out, okay? I don't care how small or silly it might seem—let me make that call."

Sobering, she nodded. "Got it." Even though given how thoroughly he was scanning their surroundings, she had a feeling he would pick up on anything suspicious way before she even had a clue. She wasn't sure why that made her nerves worse rather than better, but she was definitely on edge as they headed off along the continuation of the tire-beaten track. She was hyperaware of his walking slightly behind and off to the side of her like a big, bristling guard dog at heel. Only he was so much more than that…which made him far too distracting.

Then she saw the first thready tendrils hanging from a strangely gnarled branch, and her attention sharpened between one heartbeat and the next. She paused on the track and said softly, "Oh. Hello there." And in that instant, she felt like herself for the first time since she'd stepped through the final airport security checkpoint and into Jack Williams's world.

She was aware of his watching her and keeping close as she moved off the track and circled from one infected tree to the next, following where the tendrils grew thicker and thicker, along a wandering line that angled away from the roadway. She dragged her fingertips along the trunks but didn't touch the tendrils yet. Instead, she cataloged her impressions of the desert-dry backcountry, where the sun beat down even at its fading angle and the dust had a faint tang she couldn't quite place. *What are you?* she thought, looking up at the white strands and seeing the way the branches curled inward where they attached, becoming bent, until the most infected of the trees came to look like ancient gnomes, stooped and gnarled, with wispy white hair that trailed nearly to the ground.

"Anything I can help with?" Jack asked.

She looked back at him, startled, both because for a moment she'd almost forgotten he was there and because he actually seemed to mean it. "Actually, there is. Give me the local-level dirt on this place."

He raised an eyebrow. "How'd you figure me for a local?"

"You mentioned your father and uncle being detectives here, too. I made the leap."

That earned her a considering look before he nodded and said, "Good leap. Yep, umpteenth-generation local here. My great-something grandparents helped found the city, and there have been Williamses policing Bear Claw pretty much ever since."

"Which makes you the perfect person to fill me in on the Forgotten," she said, turning her attention back to the trees and telling herself there was no reason for her to feel a pang at the confirmation that his roots went deep.

"What do you already know?"

"Pretend I just walked in here with no advance info. You never know what's going to spark a connection."

"Yeah." He nodded. "I know how that goes. Okay, the Forgotten... Well, it's a federal buffer zone beyond the state park, too far away from civilization to interest regular campers and not challenging enough to interest the hard-core mountaineers. Doesn't have anything really in the way of natural resources or any real reason for anybody to pay attention to it, although it recently changed hands, going from federal to the city, and then almost to a public sale."

"I saw that in the file," she said, reaching up to sift her fingers through the dry, wispy strands of the parasitic fungus that was gnoming the trees, killing them. *What are you?* she asked inside. Aloud, she said, "What happened with the sale?"

"Mayor Proudfoot was pushing to sell the land to a private investor who, not surprisingly, dropped the negotiations when things broke."

"I assume you've taken a good, hard look at the investor? It would seem to me that buying the property would be to the militia's benefit."

He shot her another sidelong look. "Thought you were a plant…whatever it was."

"I've got a couple of cops in my family. You learn the thought process." Among other things.

"Well, it's not a bad theory, but the investor was legit, if an idiot. He had some geologist swearing to him that there's gold in the area, and thought he was going to put one over on the government by buying the Forgotten and striking it rich."

"I didn't think there was gold around here," she commented as they moved into a clearer area, where infected trees were more sparsely distributed among clusters of huge boulders. These trees were more severely affected than the surrounding clusters, though, which had her antenna quivering. Was there some environmental component at work?

Jack shook his head. "There isn't any gold. Just some played-out copper mines."

"Right." She had seen that from the photos, just as she had learned about the land deal from the dossier. She needed something else, something more. So, as she went into her pack for the first of the sampling kits, she said, "What about rumors, old campfire stories, that sort of thing?"

"You want to use old legends to figure out a tree disease?"

"Like I said, you never know what's going to make a connection." And, yeah, maybe she liked the sound of his voice when he wasn't being condescending, and she liked being back on her professional footing where things made sense and she didn't feel nearly so off balance, even with him only a few feet away.

"Local legends, huh? Well, depending on which story you believe, the Forgotten was either considered cursed by the native tribes in the area, or the story of the curse was whipped up later to scare people away from what was actually a hideout for the toughest of the Wild West outlaws in the decades after the Civil War."

She made a "bring it on" finger wiggle with her free hand as she tweezed fibers into a series of sterile sampling units, sealing them shut and tucking them away.

"Okay, here's how the story goes. There was once a young brave named Bear Tooth, who was smaller and weaker than his friends, and always came in last when they raced. But then one day—"

Sudden gunfire split the air, cutting him off. They were under attack!

Chapter Four

Jack reacted instantly, tackling Tori and hurling them both into the lee of the nearest boulder. His arms went around her and he muffled her scream in his chest, protecting her from the impact as they collapsed together against the stone.

Moments earlier, the fallen slab had seemed huge. Now it felt small and thin as shots rang off the far side and he anticipated the burn of a bullet crease, or worse. There was just the one shooter, but his weapon was high-powered; he was shooting from the concealment of a trio of larger rocks on higher ground; and he wasn't missing by much.

Body going into automatic mode, Jack shouldered his shotgun and snapped off two return shots that blasted off the rocks and got the guy's head down even as his mind revved with the sickening realization that the damned Shadow Militia hadn't ghosted after all…and he had led his protectee straight into an ambush.

Worse, if the guy moved and Jack didn't notice, the only thing between her and a bullet was his body. He had her crowded up against the rock. Their legs were tangled, his chest was pressed to her back and he could feel the pound of her heart and the heave of her ribs as she gasped for air.

"Don't panic," he said, bracketing the words with two

more shots and a reload. "I've got you." His hand was itching to reach for his phone, but he didn't make the grab because they were out of cell range and far away from backup. Which meant he needed her to stay calm and help him out. "Keep breathing. In and out. You got it?"

She whipped her head around and stared wildly up at him, her eyes huge and dark in her face. But he could see her struggling against the fear, see the growing determination as she nodded. "I got—"

Crack—crack—crack! The trio of shots hammered into the stone, breaking off a piece and sending something burning across Jack's upper arm. "Son of a—" he hissed.

Tori's face went stricken and she choked off a scream as she grabbed him and tried to drag him away from the point of impact. "You're hurt!"

"Barely." It was little more than a scratch really, and there would be far worse in store if he didn't do something drastic, because they were pinned down in a weaker position. Catching Tori's hands, he eased her back against the rock. "Stay," he growled, "and I mean it. Don't move. Just keep your head down."

"Where—" She clamped her lips together, pale but resolute as she followed his gaze to the track he would need to take to reach the gunman, and winced. He could get to the rocks the guy was hiding behind—he would have to get there—but it meant crossing nearly a hundred yards of open space. "You'll be a sitting duck."

"You're right." And the fact that she recognized it argued for some basic proficiency with a gun. He hoped. "Take this." He yanked his pistol, thumbed off the safety and handed it over. "When I say the word, put four bullets into those rocks up there. Space them out a little and don't worry about aiming, it's just cover fire. Just don't point it at me, okay?"

She took the weapon, surprised the hell out of him by checking it with practiced ease, though her hands shook, and looked back up at him. "Only four?"

"Save the others in case I'm not the one who comes back for you." He didn't have time to sugarcoat it, punctuated by the *crack-crack* of two more shots.

The last of the color drained from her face, but she nodded and tightened her grip on the pistol. "Make sure you are, okay?"

He slid his hand up her arm to the back of her neck and squeezed in a gesture that suddenly felt more intimate than he'd intended it to. "Will do."

Then, before he could think about all the ways this could go very wrong very fast, he popped his head around the stone, pounded two more shots into the rocks where the bastard was hiding, and then took off, staying low, moving fast, and keeping as much cover between him and the shooter as he could.

A bullet slammed into a nearby tree trunk with a fleshy, splintering noise. He ducked, dodged, snapped off a shot, saw that he was about to hit open ground and shouted, "Tori, now!"

The first shot rang out almost immediately from behind him and kicked up the gravel below the gunman's position. He didn't look to see where the second and third hit, just took off running in a jackrabbit zigzag across the open ground. His feet skidded on the loose, sandy gravel, his body burned with the anticipation of the next shot, and the rocky cover up ahead looked farther away with every step he took. But Tori's third shot came when he was halfway across, her fourth at the three-quarter's mark, and then he was there!

Breath rattling in his lungs, he dived behind the bigger boulders that led the way up to where the bastard was hiding, slammed back against the cool stone surface and made himself take the time to reload, even though his heart was slamming with the rhythm of *get him, get him, get him!*

Determination gripped him—anger, even. It wasn't coming just from the drive for justice that was part of the Williams DNA either, wasn't because of the troubles that had been hammering at Bear Claw and its overworked, understaffed P.D. either. It was bubbling straight up from deep inside him: a raw and atavistic need to make sure nothing happened to Tori.

Growling low in his throat, he charged up the hill, staying low and moving fast, sacrificing some stealth and cover for speed because he was all too aware that the gunman hadn't gotten off a shot in nearly a minute.

He led with his shotgun, swung around the last outcropping—and stopped dead at the sight of an empty, scuffed-up spot where the shooter had been.

Tori! He shouted the word in his skull but didn't let it out as he spun in a quick three-sixty, not sure if the guy had gone after her or taken off. *Please, let him have taken off.*

There was no sign of the gunman save for the scuff marks leading down, a single line where the guy had re-traced his trail and then branched off—straight onto a wide, rocky ledge that didn't hold any tracks and was headed straight for Tori.

Pulse thudding in ears that strained for the sound of

gunfire, Jack charged along the ridge of stone, and then crept to within a few boulders of where he'd left Tori, hoping to hell that the silence meant she was hiding, not taken hostage. The last few seconds were the worst, as he got to within a single stone of her position, straining to see if he could detect the sounds of one or two people on the other side. Then, knowing it was better to risk his position than take friendly fire, he called softly, "Tori, it's Jack. I—"

A blur came at him from the side. He wheeled with his gun up and ready, then jerked it to the side as his brain registered petite curves and huge brown eyes. There wasn't time to notice much else before she flung herself against him and hung on tight, all warmth and curves and slightness against him.

Even as he told himself to detach and go after the guy, his arms closed around her with equal force.

"You're okay!" Her words were muffled in his shirt and her body vibrated with tension. "I thought..." As if suddenly realizing what she'd done, she pushed away from him, blushing. "Here, take this." She shoved the pistol into his free hand, leaving him standing there with a gun in each hand and the imprint of her body on his as she took a couple more steps back, holding her hands out to her sides as if to say "Sorry, don't know what got into me."

And even though he knew the moment had come from fear and relief, part of him was dying to close the gap between them and touch her for real.

Bad timing, he told himself. *And a really, really bad idea.* So instead of reaching for her, he safetied and holstered the pistol, then turned away from her to scan the scene. "Did you see him?"

"He's gone?"

"Looks like it." And sure enough, a quick but thorough search of the immediate area said that the gunman had left. Jack wasn't willing to bet on how far he'd gone, though, or that he wasn't coming back with reinforcements, so he turned them back the way they had come, feeling the prickle of unseen—maybe imagined, maybe not—eyes on the back of his neck. "Let's get out of here."

"Hang on." Tori dug in. "I need my bag."

He might have argued—his gut said they had to get out of there fast—but the sudden gleam in her eyes told him that he'd be wasting his time. Besides, it wasn't much of a detour over to where her knapsack had fallen...and he wasn't sure how much of his disquiet came from the gunman and how much from feeling that he and Tori were skirting the edge of dangerous territory...especially given that her stay in Bear Claw had a guaranteed expiration date, and he wasn't wired for "casual."

Still, though, as he led her back to the SUV using a different track than the one they'd taken before, just in case, he was acutely aware not just of their surroundings and the unusually quiet tension in the air, but also of her. The practiced moves of her body said she was used to moving silently through the woods, but the slight hitch in her breathing said she was terrified and doing her best to hold it together.

On the drive earlier, he had been thinking that she was too slight to handle the Forgotten, skilled or not. Now, his respect notched up—she could handle herself and then some. Still, he wished like hell that he'd talked her out of the trip. She shouldn't have been in the line of fire, period.

That was fixable, though. He would get her back down

to civilization, load her onto a plane, and get back to work. There was no way Tucker could keep him off this investigation now, not when—

"Oh, hell." He stopped dead at the sight of the SUV. It was still sitting where he'd parked it, but the hood was popped. "Stay put," he ordered grimly, "and get ready with that pistol."

"Shouldn't we stick together?"

"Not if… Not right now." If the damn thing was wired to blow, he didn't want her anywhere near it—and the militia had done worse. Without taking his eyes off their surroundings, he dug into his jacket for a canteen and his pocketknife. "Hold on to these for me, will you? If we get separated, I want you to head back down. Stay off the road but keep it in sight."

"You…" She trailed off, then caught his hand for a moment, squeezed it. "Don't do that to me, okay?"

"I'll do my best." They shared a look that lasted a beat too long to be for simple luck, and then he pulled away. "Cover me. If something that's not me moves, shoot it. I'd rather lose a deer than our lives."

Without another word, he slipped out into the open and headed for the SUV. To his surprise, Tori melted almost immediately into the trees; he couldn't see her even though he knew exactly where to look. Damn. His respect notched up another bit, and along with it his determination not to let her down.

Steady, he told himself as he got to within a few feet of the SUV. *Don't rush it.* But he was also very aware of the first blush of pink on the horizon, heralding the too-quick autumn dusk. He had the equipment for them to camp out, sure, but not in the face of a potential armed standoff, or worse.

Forcing himself to focus, he scanned the vehicle. He didn't see a tripwire or evidence of explosives, although with today's miniaturization, that was no guarantee. But he was losing light and his gut said they had to get moving. So, holding his breath, he opened the hood.

"Son of a—" He bit off the curse, then ran the hood the rest of the way open, staring dismayed at the mess of wires and hoses that had taken the sharp end of a knife. Which made sense, he realized after the fact: assuming that the gunman had stumbled over them, he wouldn't have been carrying explosives or tripwires. But he'd obviously had a knife with him, and he'd probably be coming back with the other stuff.

Lifting his hand, he beckoned Tori in from the tree line. She looked at him hopefully as she approached, but must have seen something in his eyes, because her face was grim by the time she joined him at the SUV.

"I think I can cobble things back together with the supplies I've got on hand," he said. Hopefully his patches would last long enough to get them back down to the station, or at least into radio range of help. "I need you to keep watch from the trees while I work on this."

"Not from here?"

He thought about sugar coating it, but went with the bald truth instead. "Matt and Gigi were nearly killed when the militia nailed their Jeep with a rocket-propelled grenade."

Her eyes whipped back to him. "In other words, we're sitting ducks."

"Which is why I need you in the trees."

She opened her mouth to protest, then snapped it shut once more. Nodded. "Of course." Then she surprised him by catching his hand and tugging him down, to brush a kiss across his cheek. "Thank you."

"It's my job," he said automatically, as he had done pretty much since his first days as a rook when someone wanted to thank him. This time, though, his skin heated and he found himself wanting to say something more even though he didn't have a clue what that might be. Then she pulled away and headed for the trees, walking almost silently and keeping her eyes moving.

Damn, she impressed him.

No distractions, he reminded himself, and rummaged in the SUV for the wire stripper and a fat roll of electrical tape before he turned back to the slashed hoses and wires. This time, though, he focused wholly on the job, trusting that his partner—or, rather, his protectee—had his back. And given the list of rooks he'd been working with over the past couple of years thanks to Mayor Skinflint, it had been a long time since he'd had anyone watching his six for real. It should've rubbed wrong that it was a scientist he could practically blow over…but it didn't.

He'd think about that later, though. Like after they were the hell out of there and she was on a plane headed home.

"This one goes to this one…" He talked himself through the patches, working too quickly to really be methodical, but not letting himself make any mistakes because there wasn't any time for a do-over. He was barely two-thirds of the way through when he realized he was squinting to see, and had to click on a small flashlight and hold it between his teeth.

All the while, the back of his neck was strung tight

waiting for the sound of a footstep or the crack of a gun-shot. He was sweating by the time he taped the last connection into place. Then, sending up a wordless prayer, he leaned across the driver's seat and tried the key.

The engine turned over and started to come to life, but then coughed and died. "Come on, come on," he muttered, slinging himself into the seat and risking a glance over to the tree line. Tori was just barely visible within the branches. She flashed him a thumbs up and mouthed *You can do it,* then faded back into the branches, leaving him to think she had stepped into view just for him.

Shaking his head, he tried the key again, goosing the gas a little. The SUV started, and this time it stayed running. *"Nice!"*

He waved to Tori as he lunged out of the vehicle to slam the hood, heart suddenly pounding where he'd been mostly calm up to this point. So close. They were so damn close to getting out of there! She burst from the trees, moving fast but still quiet, gripping his pistol two-handed and somehow managing to look simultaneously terrified and utterly capable as she piled into the SUV from the other side and banged the door shut with a slam that was gunshot-loud after all the quiet.

Pulse racing, he met her eyes. "Here goes nothing." Only it was really everything as he shifted into gear, the transmission synched up and he hit the gas…and everything worked the way it was supposed to. He didn't realize he was holding his breath until it came out in a big whoosh. "Come on," he muttered under his breath. "Hang in there."

Tori didn't say a word, just kept the pistol in her lap and her eyes moving, scanning the passing scrub. But she reached over with her free hand and briefly gripped his wrist in thanks.

For Jack, the next few hours passed in a blur of death-gripping the steering wheel, squinting to tell the faint tread-marked trail from the surrounding unstable shale, and hoping to hell his patches would hold. He and Tori exchanged a few words now and then on the practicalities, and once they were out of the Forgotten, she set aside the pistol, turned up the heat and sagged against her door, her eyes still moving, watching for trouble even in the moonlit darkness.

They both knew that if there was going to be a problem at this point, they likely wouldn't see it coming. The SUV's headlights lit the night with an "aim the RPG here" sign in neon, but it wasn't like he could turn them off. He was having a devil of a time staying on the trail as it was. So he drove, wincing with every bounce and bang, imagining his patches loosening up and the hoses teetering on the brink of separation.

He was strung out, his eyes burning, his body caught in a surreal state of exhausted terror that had him hallucinating as he tried his damnedest to see the track. That had to be a hallucination, because there was no way—

Tori jolted and straightened. "It's the tower! We made it!"

He blinked hard, then had to blink again to clear his burning eyes, but the lights didn't disappear along with the gritty fog shrouding his vision. They stayed true—small, amber pinpricks that expanded to glows and then became the solar floodlights that topped the observatory.

Station Fourteen had never looked so good.

"We could walk it from here," he rasped, feeling the tension draining away, leaving him nearly limp with relief.

"Let's not and say we did," she said drily. Then she flashed him a grin, her eyes gleaming with the same mad joy that was suddenly pumping through him.

He snorted, guffawed, cracked up. And they rolled into the parking lot laughing like a pair of idiots.

The second he took his foot off the gas and hit the brake, though, the engine thudded and died. Kaput. Done.

He choked off the tension-relieving laughter, letting it bleed away in a long sigh. "Holy crap, Tori. We made it."

She reached across and gripped his wrist as she had done before, only this time she let her hand linger. "We only made it because of you. Thank you, Jack. I…" She shook her head. "Thank you."

The old "just doing my job" got stuck in his throat, locked there by the flare of heat that kindled at the point where she was touching him and rolled up his arm to fill his chest. He just shook his head, not even sure what he was denying anymore as he turned his grip inside hers to thread their fingers together and tug her closer.

She could have pretended not to understand, could've pulled away. She didn't do either of those things, though. Instead, as the breath backed up in his lungs and the warmth turned to a gnawing ache mixed with flames, she leaned toward him in the darkness. He lifted his other hand and drew his fingers along the side of her face and back to brush her hair behind one ear, giving her one last chance to retreat. She didn't, though.

And so, in a broken-down SUV that had died in the back of beyond, he broke the rules he'd spent most of his adult life figuring out—three dates to a kiss, at least ten to take it further, everything slow and methodical, and designed to test the compatibility and long-term potential of each match. This wasn't the third date, wasn't even a date, but he didn't care. All he cared about was kissing Tori.

Chapter Five

As Jack's lips touched hers, Tori decided that she didn't care that he was a cop and a local; she only cared that he was solid and warm against her. His mouth was firm, his grip demanding even though she knew he would let her go if she pulled away.

She crowded closer instead, and parted her lips to taste him.

A groan rumbled in his chest as their tongues touched and slid, and her soft moan echoed beneath the sound, coming from the sharp, masculine flavor and the heat that seared through her, surrounded her. He was there, he was *real,* and that was a shock to the senses in the wake of the last few hours, which felt suddenly unreal, as if they had happened to someone else, or came from a movie about shootouts, sabotaged vehicles and car chases.

The man kissing her was equally outside of her normal zone, as were the heat and desire rocketing through her, but she could grab on to those feelings, dig into his solid strength and feel *alive*. They had made it out, made it down. They were okay, thanks to him. If he hadn't been there... She shuddered against him, feeling safe and protected.

But at the same time she was very aware that this, too,

was a moment out of reality, fleeting and temporary. It had to be. So when her hands wanted to clutch, she made them caress instead, and when his body stiffened and he made a low noise of surprise, she let go and leaned back, hands up and open in the universal gesture of "don't freak, no harm, no foul."

That was how she ran each and every one of her short-term relationships, after all: no harm, no foul.

They sat there a moment, in a pool of light coming from the observatory's floods, staring at each other. His breathing was fast, his eyes hot with a desire that speared straight into her and made her want to fling herself at him, on him, kiss him until neither of them was thinking about anything but the slip and slide of flesh and the pounding of their hearts.

But even though his eyes were hot, he shook his head slowly as if to clear it, or maybe deny what had just happened between them. And although that rejection pinched at her feminine core, she was the one who'd let go first, and she was the one who broke the suddenly strained silence to say, "Sorry. Got caught up in the moment there."

He searched her face for an interval that stretched long enough for her to wonder what he was looking for, what he saw. But he only said, "We should get inside and start making calls. The guys at the station house need to hear about what just happened, as do the members of the task force; I need backup, and you need an official escort back down to the city."

The implication was "and a plane ticket the hell out of here," and she wasn't arguing—there was a line between dedication and stupidity, and sticking around when she was being shot at would put her way over onto the "stupid" side.

THE RINGING PHONE brought Percy Proudfoot groggily awake. As he fumbled on the nightstand for his cell, he muttered, "Damn it." He slept alone, so there was nobody to care if he kept up his cursing when he knocked the phone off the nightstand and onto the floor and had to get down there and hunt for the damn thing. And if the staffers who lived in the other wing of the mayoral mansion heard anything, they'd been well-paid to turn a deaf ear to far stranger sounds.

The Aubusson carpet scuffed his bare knees and he nearly brained himself on the corner of the nightstand, but he came up with the phone and leaned back against the giant canopy bed to flip it open. There was no ID on the display, just a number, but when he saw that it was coming in on his most private line, the sleepy cobwebs disappeared.

Taking a deep breath, he clicked the call live and answered with a professional, borderline respectful, "Proudfoot here."

It wouldn't do any good to irritate the man on the other end of the line. He was powerful, far-reaching, and he had Percy's mayoral future in a vise.

"You said you'd keep the cops away from the Forgotten." The Investor—that was what he'd told Percy to call him from the very start of their association—sounded more than irritated. He sounded coldly furious. Murderous, even.

Uh-oh. Going on instant alert, Percy searched his memory banks for even a hint of trouble, and drew a blank. "I did. They are. Chief Mendoza pulled his people off the militia investigation and prioritized the drug case last week. There's nothing going on out in the Forgotten."

"You're out of the loop, Mayor. There was a cop there today, Jack Williams, along with a woman scientist."

"Bull. They wouldn't—" But given his increasingly strained relationship with the Bear Claw P.D., it was possible that they *had* cut him out. Or rather, that they had delayed crucial info as long as possible, knowing he would clamp down on anything that sounded expensive. Ice chased through his veins and he went into damage control mode. "What happened?"

"One of my scouts found their vehicle and tracked them into the hot zone. They were less than a mile away from the encampment when he found them. Unfortunately, he couldn't pin them down, and his comm malfunctioned, so he had to go back on foot for help, and by the time he returned with a team, they were gone. Which means they made it back down to the city most likely, and you don't have much time to clamp down on whatever kind of a response your people are putting together. And I mean clamp down, Proudfoot. The Forgotten is my territory, bought and paid for."

"I know. I... Damn it." Percy's mind raced as he sorted through his options, knowing he would have to be very careful right now, not just to get the Investor's needs met, but his own as well. There was an election coming up, after all. If he spun this right...yeah. He could make it work. "Okay, I can handle this, no problem. But I could use your help..."

WITHIN A COUPLE of hours of Jack calling in the attack, Tucker and several other cops were up at the observatory taking statements and starting the process of reorganizing the Shadow Militia task force. At least that was the plan, but then things started to get strange.

"Well, this puts a new spin on things," Tucker said, his expression thoughtful as he clicked off his phone—which was the only satellite-enabled phone the P.D. had managed to fund, despite repeated requests.

"A guy seriously walked in off the street, handed over his hunting rifle and confessed to going after me and Tori?" Jack asked, having picked up the gist from his boss's side of the conversation.

They were sitting in the downstairs main room of the observatory, Jack on one of the sofas, Tucker in a big club chair. Tori was upstairs and, outside, the floodlit parking area was starting to get busy, as more cops and feds arrived and the militia task force started assembling prior to making the trek out to the Forgotten at first light.

Except now it sounded like it might not have been the militia after all.

Tucker nodded. "A drifter named Wayne Gibbs. He's got priors in California for aggravated assault, is strongly antigovernment, and says he's been camping in a cave a little ways away from where you and Tori were searching. As far as he's concerned, he was just protecting his homestead. And, yeah, he's got a prescription for antipsychotics that hasn't been filled since summer."

"Damn." Jack shook his head, not just because it sounded too convenient, but also because he could actually see it. Hell, he *had* seen it: a couple of years earlier, there had been a similar case when an ex-marine decided the country owed him some land. The guy had moved his camper and his junkyard dog onto a chunk of land near Station Eight and claimed squatter's rights, then went after a couple of rangers with his shotgun when they tried to run him off.

And that wasn't the only instance of people squatting on state and federal land in the area either. Between the economy and the loss of most of Bear Claw's homeless shelters due to budget cuts, there were more and more indigents trying to scratch a living wherever they could, including the state park.

They were usually found pretty quickly, though. Which begged the question, "Why did it take us this long to notice him?"

Tucker lifted a shoulder. "We're looking into it, but the last serious scan was a couple of weeks ago. Could be that he just hasn't been there that long."

Jack blew out a breath. "Okay, so if we say it wasn't the militia, then what does that mean for me and…Dr. Bay?" He stumbled when *me and Tori* sounded way too intimate within the confines of his skull.

He'd made sure to keep things coolly professional when Tucker had arrived and immediately called her downstairs to go over the attack. He'd kept his report by the book while trying to keep his mind off their kiss…but it'd been almost impossible when he could still—even now—remember exactly how she tasted, how her surprising curves had melted against him, how her breath had caught in her throat when he touched her.

He'd told himself over and over again that they were both adults and a simple kiss—even one that was way off his usual schedule—didn't have to change anything between them, especially given her "I'm backing away now, and we don't have to talk about this" reaction. But the thing was, he couldn't stop thinking that it *had* changed something. Because now he was almost preternaturally attuned to her, entirely aware that she was upstairs working on her samples, that she had showered and changed and that she hadn't met his eyes more than twice after the kiss.

"Well, if the shooter wasn't part of the militia—" Tucker began, only to have his phone start ringing again. "Hold that thought." He answered, listened and blew out a breath before he said, "Yeah, okay. Thanks." He didn't look thrilled as he clicked off, though. With a glance at Jack, he said, "Her people are putting the investigation on hold. They don't like their scientists being shot at."

"Didn't much enjoy it myself," Jack said, but the attempt at a quip fell seriously flat. "They're pulling her out?"

It was the logical thing to do. So why did his instincts say it was the wrong decision?

Tucker nodded. "It'll simplify things at any rate."

"Maybe not," Tori's voice said from behind Jack. "Because things just got more complicated, at least on my end."

He turned, realizing that he wasn't surprised to see her there; part of him had sensed her, had known she was near. Standing halfway up the spiral staircase with a mini laptop in her arms, she was wearing jeans and a blue-green zip-up hoodie, and had traded the boots for beaded moccasins with polka-dotted socks that added an unexpected touch of whimsy. There was no whimsy in her face, though. She was pale, drawn and resolute.

"Did you find something in the samples?" Tucker asked with a pained expression that suggested the antacids would have gone down real good right then.

She nodded. "To put it bluntly, you're in deep trouble here. The fungus is spreading exponentially, and it's poised at a threshold value right now. A few more days, a week at the most, and you're not going to be talking about just one section of the forest anymore."

Jack wanted to say *You're kidding,* but he could tell from her expression that she was deadly serious. "All of the Forgotten will be infected that quickly?"

"Not just the Forgotten. The entire state park."

"The... Hell." The park wasn't just one of the three biggest tourist attractions in the city, underpinning the economy; it was Bear Claw Canyon State Park, and it was home.

As she crossed to the seating area, Tucker pinched the bridge of his nose. "Tell me you're not serious."

"I'm serious. Here." She sank down to the sofa beside Jack, her weight barely denting the cushions as she leaned forward and set the notebook computer on the glass-topped coffee table. "Watch this." She tapped a few keys and a satellite image of the Bear Claw region popped onto the screen. When she hit Play, a small red patch appeared near the river that cut across the northeast quadrant of the Forgotten. "The first survey done a month ago." The red expanded like blood from a wound. "The second survey." More red. "Today...and this is what's going to happen if we don't suppress this thing." It took three slides for things to go from bad to worse—to a bloodbath.

"Damn," Jack muttered. "Are you sure?"

"I'm confident in the data and the simulation, but we're talking about Mother Nature here. She's capable of endlessly surprising us humans. Sometimes for the better, sometimes not."

"We can't bet on Bear Claw Canyon for hoping for a surprise." Jack reached across to rerun the simulation. "And we're not just talking about the trees either, are we?"

Tucker's bleak expression went bleaker. "We're not?"

"The trees help anchor the ecosystem," Tori answered, and gave him a quick run-through of the summary she had given Jack earlier.

"Damn it." Tucker shook his head as if trying to deny the inevitable. "The Park Service has put the investigation on hold until we're sure it's safe for Dr. Bay to be out in the Forgotten."

"Tori, please."

"Tori, then."

"Aren't we already sure?" Jack asked. "You've got the shooter in custody." Even as he said it, the voice of reason inside him was saying *What are you doing?* And it had a point: he should take the out he was being offered and be grateful for it. But at Tori's questioning look, he briefed her on the gunman's confession, then added, "A team will go up there in the morning and check out his story, but if he seems legit, then it was just a random attack, not evidence that the Shadow Militia is still in the area."

But Tucker wasn't convinced. "I've got my orders, which are to put Tori on a plane out of here and put every available cop on the drug case, pronto. The boss didn't even want us to bother corroborating the confession, just wanted to run with it."

"Tell him that the disease is poised to hit the rest of the park," Tori urged.

Tucker agreed, although he didn't look convinced that it would make a difference. As he made the call, Tori went upstairs to explain to her bosses that it looked like the shooting wasn't related to the militia and, moreover, that the outbreak was a bigger problem than they had thought. But even as Tucker clicked off his phone, shaking his head, Tori came back into the room glowering. "They're insisting that I've got enough sample material to work with back at the lab, and that regardless of why the shooting occurred, the situation is too 'volatile'—" she scorned the word with finger quotes "—for me to risk it."

"They're not necessarily wrong," Jack said. "You could have been killed today."

"But I wasn't," she countered. "And they're wrong about the samples. Sure, I've got enough to get started, but I never know what I'm going to need until I actually get into the work itself. I need to be here, need to have access to the Forgotten if I'm going to have any chance at all to get ahead of this outbreak before it reaches critical mass."

Tucker spread his hands. "I tried, but Mendoza isn't budging. The official investigation into the outbreak is over for right now."

Her eyes blazed. "You'll have to drag me out of… Wait a minute. You said that the *official* investigation is over. Does that mean I can stay up here on my own time?"

"Not without an escort, and I can't officially spare anyone to stay up here with you."

There was that word again: *official*. Jack heard the hint loud and clear.

So did Tori. Without missing a beat, she turned to him. "Will you stay with me…unofficially?"

"I…" *Damn.* It wasn't a surprise that she asked—of course she had asked. She'd do whatever it took to stay on the job, and she had the tenacity of a top-notch cop.

What surprised him was the fact that he was torn, not because he was attracted to her or because they had kissed, but because she needed to be there. And because, despite everything that had happened today, being out there with her had reminded him that he had always loved the backcountry.

He'd grown up roaming the great outdoors with his father and brothers, had escaped to the mountains during college and his rookie years, letting the fresh air and open skies clear his head and remind him that most of his day-to-day hassles could be easily outweighed by the sight of an eagle soaring overhead or the satisfaction his inner caveman got from fishing for his dinner and cooking it over an open campfire. And even the bad stuff that wasn't totally outweighed—and as a cop he'd seen more than his share of the wretched and unforgivable things humans could do to each other—had lost some of its teeth when he was up in the backcountry.

The trips had tapered off and then gone away as he'd grown up, though, and he hadn't realized until today just how much he missed it. There was a sense of freedom out there, a wildness that called to something inside him so strongly that he didn't know how he'd gone so long without recognizing the lack in his life. Hell, he'd been up to Station Fourteen and the Forgotten a handful of times in the past few months, first investigating the attempted murder of a park ranger, then the Shadow Militia. Back then, he'd scanned the crime scenes without seeing beyond the job. Today, for the first time in far too long, he had done his job but seen the beauty, too.

He couldn't let that be destroyed. But he also couldn't forget about the dozens of people who had already been hurt by the Death Stare, the hundreds more that could be affected if the cops didn't get a handle on the drug trade, pronto.

"I can ask Matt to recommend someone to escort Tori," Tucker said. "A couple of the rangers are ex-cops or ex-military, and they know the backcountry."

"So do I," Jack grated. More, he knew a bit about Tori, and how her combination of guts and dedication could get her in trouble. And he knew that he didn't want anyone else watching out for her. He didn't believe in instant connections—at least not of the man-woman kind—but that didn't stop him from wanting to be the guy out there with her, making sure that nothing bad happened to her while she was in Bear Claw.

Tori held his eyes. "I'd feel better if it's you out there with me."

Damn it. To Tucker, he said, "You'll square it with Mendoza, right? It's not like he really wants to see my face right now anyway."

Tucker nodded. "I'll put you in for vacation, say you needed more time."

At Tori's look, Jack shook his head. The sting of guilt at turning down a chance to get back on the Death Stare case was his problem, not hers.

To Tucker, he said, "Do it." To Tori, he said, "Looks like you've got yourself an escort, Dr. Bay." And anybody who wanted to hurt her was going to have to go through him to do it.

Chapter Six

Two days later, as she sat in her small room under the eaves of the observatory talking to her head lab tech via webcam, Tori finally started feeling like she was getting somewhere with the investigation.

"I've got those sequencing results you were waiting on," Chondra's voice and image said from the screen of her laptop. "It's a big file. The download may take a minute."

"Especially given that I'm in the middle of nowhere," Tori agreed wryly. But although the signal was patchy and there was a good chance she could lose the uplink at any second, she was grateful to have even that much.

Overall, life out at Station Fourteen hadn't been as onerous as she had initially feared. She and Jack had dropped off the grid without major problems, and they'd been up to the Forgotten twice more. Granted, there had been some hairy moments—there always were on a field assignment—but nothing she couldn't handle. And if once or twice she'd thought she saw movement in the distance, or it felt like someone was watching her, that was just the power of suggestion, just as the two times the motion sensors had gone off in the middle of the night, causing Jack to closet her safely away while he searched the observatory, had been false alarms caused by the wind or an animal of some sort.

She hadn't let that distract her, though, because the forest needed her…which was why she'd pulled in some favors and gotten some off-the-books help from some truly excellent researchers, including Chondra.

Tall and statuesque, with dark skin and exotic lavender eyes, Chondra looked more like the former high-fashion model she'd been than the master's-level biochemical analyst she'd become. Heck, she made even a lab coat look fashionable, with a tuck here and a twist there that showed off her generous curves with a tasteful femininity not normally possessed by a garment that made Tori look like she was wearing a pup tent backward.

But despite the gap in "it" factor, Tori and Chondra were fast friends—and she had leaned on that friendship without hesitation or remorse when the university had backed up the Park Service's decision to pull her off the Bear Claw case, forcing her to take personal time and cutting her off from the lab's resources…at least in theory. In reality, over the two days since she and Jack had both gone more or less rogue, her lab mates had clocked in dozens of hours on the Bear Claw infection, taking things to the next level by fragmenting the genetic material of the fungus and shotgun sequencing it in an effort to figure out the parasite's nearest evolutionary relatives, in hope that that would lead them to a preventive measure, or even a cure. Because so far, just as the prior research teams had found, the fungus was resistant to all the usual suspects when it came to treating this sort of thing.

An icon came to life on Tori's screen, indicating that the download was complete. "I've got it." Aware of the gleam in Chondra's eyes and her air of suppressed excitement, Tori had to stop herself from holding her breath as she clicked on the file. She skimmed through the basic information on the sequencing—how many fragments had been run for an average of how many base pairs of sequence information, blah, blah, blah—and then stopped dead when she got to the alignment results. "Wait. What?"

Chondra laughed. "I'm pretty sure that's exactly what I said when I saw it."

"That doesn't make any sense." According to the sequencing data, the three best hits—the species with the highest DNA sequence similarities to their unknown contributor—came from members of the amatias and bromeliads, and a rare strain of pseudomonas. In other words, they had a poisonous mushroom, an air plant and a deep-sea bacterium.

What the hell?

The amatias were among the most poisonous of mushrooms, and hadn't even been on her list of possible ancestors for the Bear Claw organism. The bromeliads were the tropical air plants found in Mexico, Central America and South America, in habitats ranging from rainforests to souvenir shops. Which accounted for the white filaments—sort of—but didn't explain how the two had come to be in the same sample, or why the third-best hit was a deep-sea bacterium that lived near sulfur vents.

Even more astoundingly, the hits didn't overlap; instead, the matches came from different places in the DNA of the Bear Claw fungus, suggesting that the parasite infecting the Forgotten was somehow a hybrid of the three.

Tori just sat there for a few seconds, blinking and trying to assimilate the information. "Well, that's…weird."

"Hello, understatement." Chondra's eyes gleamed. "Based on the DNA, it's an entirely new species. That means you get to name it, right?"

"If it's a new species, yes. If it's a science project gone awry, then, no." It wouldn't be the first time that scientists had engineered a hybrid species and then lost control of it.

There were strictly enforced regulations designed to prevent such things, of course, but Mother Nature had ways of getting around humankind's attempts to control her. Just as the gypsy moths and starlings had been accidentally introduced to North America and took over their ecological niches, different strains of bioengineered plants had "escaped" from their test fields and outcompeted the native strains to take over. In most cases, the damage had been contained. Perhaps not in this one, though.

"A science—oh." Chondra's mouth stayed round in surprise for a moment, and then she rolled her eyes up and slapped her forehead. "Duh, why didn't I think of that?"

"Probably because you're doing your own official lab work in addition to the queries I keep piling on you," Tori said, "and you're running ragged." Lord knows, *she* was, though not for the same reason. She thrived on being overworked, and usually did fine on just a few hours of sleep per night when she was off on an assignment. Now, though, she was low on sleep, but not because of work. Instead, she had spent the past two nights tossing and turning restlessly, all too aware of the man sleeping on the floor below, and the fact that there wasn't anybody else around for miles.

And she so wasn't going there.

Forcing herself back on track—it was bad enough she was asking Chondra and a couple of the others to sneak around to help her out, worse if she was only giving the conversation half her attention—she said, "See if you can find out who might have been doing work like this, and what they were trying to accomplish. Don't contact them, though. Just get me the names."

Chondra's eyes widened fractionally. "You're going to turn them in?"

"I'm going to do whatever gets me a handle on controlling this thing the fastest. The forest is the priority here, not the politics." At least for right now. Once she'd dealt with the Forgotten, she would blow the whistle on the culprits. Because losing track of a genetically engineered organism—especially one that she suspected would be highly toxic to humans, based on the amatia DNA—and then failing to call the proper authorities wasn't just irresponsible, it was criminal.

"Anything else?"

"How is June coming with that life-cycle analysis?" Another of Tori's techs—and also a trusted friend—had pitched in immediately when she heard what was going on. She had been analyzing different samples, trying to figure out how the fungus—or fungus hybrid?—reproduced, and how its youngest stages spread.

In several sections of the Forgotten, Tori had found areas where the fungal growth was far thinner and younger-seeming than that in the surrounding areas, as if an acre or so of the stuff had died off and then been re-seeded onto the trees. She was hoping that if they could figure out why the die-offs were happening, then she might be able to trigger a more widespread killing of the fungus.

Maybe. Hopefully.

"Her preliminary report should be in your email," Chondra answered. "As far as I know, she hadn't cracked the die-offs yet, though she'd got some info on the spores."

"And not good info," Tori muttered after pulling up the report and scanning the first few lines. "They're fire-resistant." Which meant that torching the Forgotten with a series of controlled burns designed to wipe out the sick trees wouldn't take care of the problem. If anything, that would make it worse by sending the protected spores into the air.

"We'll keep on it," Chondra said. "There's an answer. We just need to make sure we're asking the right questions."

"And based on the sequencing data, those questions might be less about natural life cycles and more about which labs have been trying to engineer a potentially toxic, definitely parasitic fungus that contains sulfur-bacteria DNA." Tori shook her head. "This is getting weird."

"As far as I'm concerned, it got weird the second some guy took a potshot at you and you didn't get on the first plane coming home." Chondra crossed her arms and gave a disapproving look. "Are you sure you don't have enough to come back and run this from the lab?"

Tori shook her head. "I'm sure, and there's no more danger really. The guy's story checked out, cave and all." And the other stuff was just false alarms and an overactive imagination.

"That doesn't explain why you still need to be there."

"I just do, that's all. Something's telling me to stay put, and over the years I've learned to listen to my gut on stuff like this."

But as Tori said goodbye and ended the transmission,

she hoped she had sounded far more convincing than she felt. Because, really, she didn't have a clue whether the urge to stay was coming from her instincts as a researcher, or from something far more primal and way less logical— namely, desire.

She might be a plant researcher, but she was plenty familiar with animal attraction. And although she and Jack had kept a very professional distance after that one kiss— that one crazy kiss—there was an added sizzle between them now.

It wasn't solely physical either, nor was it leftover gratitude from him having saved her butt. Instead, it had turned out that they actually kind of liked each other. Not to mention that they worked well together, with him offering help when she needed it and backing off when she didn't, and once or twice stepping in when he thought she was straying over the line of safety. Although their conversations had mostly centered on her investigation, she had gotten him to share a few memories of his childhood adventures in the forest, and she had told a story or two on herself, mostly mishaps during field investigations. And despite her intentions to focus on the case and not her hottie bodyguard, she found herself looking forward to the drive there and back, when they were closed in together, breathing the same air and darting sidelong looks when each thought the other wasn't looking.

She was thirty-one and at the top of her game, careerwise. She had a great lab, solid funding, good classes to teach and a hugely flexible travel schedule. There was nothing about her life she wanted to change right now.

But she couldn't get Jack out of her mind. Normally, that wouldn't have been an issue—although she didn't change her men quite as often as she changed her locale, she'd had more than her share of fieldwork flings. Even given the potentially serious threat she was dealing with here, she could have made the time for some fun.

Jack, though, didn't seem to consider dating—or, in her case, hooking up—as anything remotely approaching fun. The few times they had skirted the edges of the issue in conversation, he'd made it plenty clear that he wasn't interested in quick and casual, and that he had some heavy thoughts when it came to relationships.

Not that there was anything wrong with that, to coin a Seinfeld-ism, but it wasn't her style by a long shot, which meant that it wasn't smart for her to remember their kiss… and it definitely wasn't smart for her to wonder what it would feel like to take it further.

Still, smart or not, dozens of butterflies dipped and spun inside her as she headed down the spiral staircase to the lower level, and they got worse when she caught a whiff of red sauce and garlic and heard cookware clanging softly over the refrain from "Home on the Range."

Oh, God. He was cooking. And humming. The two together tipped her a little further from "like" to "lust" and warning bells went off.

Pausing on the lowest rung of the stairs, she told herself to go back upstairs and chow down on the camping rations she kept in her bag for emergencies. But she was starving and she was a sucker for pasta.

Her feet were moving before her brain had fully weighed the decision. And before she could second-guess herself, she was in the kitchen doorway, and he was turning to greet her with a raised eyebrow that said he'd heard her on the stairs and knew how long she'd stood there debating.

He'd stopped humming, leaving the kitchen filled with the sounds of boiling water, bubbling sauce, and the low-pitched churn of the vent over the stove…and nothing else, as they stood there, staring at each other. After a moment, he said, "This doesn't need to be weird. I wanted spaghetti and apparently Matt and Gigi don't believe in the jarred stuff. So because I was cooking, I made enough for two plus leftovers. You want some or you don't want some, that's cool. You want to take it upstairs, go for it. Or we could sit down and share a meal. Your call."

A smart woman would have gone with takeout. Tori, though, grinned and said, "I'm starving and it smells great. Let's eat."

THEY STUCK CAREFULLY to neutral subjects as they ate—the case, her work, Bear Claw and a handful of other topics suited to a couple of relative strangers who didn't need to get to know each other because they were only in each other's lives very fleetingly. And if the careful neutrality of it irritated Jack, rubbing at the raw, edgy parts of him that had been worn down past the point of restraint by two days of being out in the wilderness with a woman who wasn't like anyone he'd ever thought he would go for, yet had gotten thoroughly under his skin, he held himself in check, reminding himself of all the reasons he'd decided not to go there.

He needed to focus on protecting her and she needed to focus on saving Bear Claw Canyon, and as distracting as the tension might be between them, the alternative would be even more distracting. Problem was, he was starting to wonder just how much protection she really needed. Because aside from a couple of false alarms, the Forgotten had proven remarkably tame, and she was fully capable out in the backcountry—more than capable really.

While she might not have hiked circles around him—his longer reach and greater strength gave him the advantage in places—she'd held her own out in the Forgotten, clambering out on edgy precipices and high into the gnarled limbs of the sickened trees to get the samples she wanted. She had brushed him off a few times when he'd wanted to rein her in, but her instincts had proven good and he'd eventually backed off even further.

With the shooter's story checking out and no concrete sign of the Shadow Militia—though he was keeping a damn sharp eye out—he'd had far too much time to think about other things. Like the Death Stare case…and Tori. She wasn't like anyone he'd ever known before—an intriguing mix of occasional shyness when it came to him, guts when it came to just about everything else…including, it seemed, relationships.

Their lives were completely different, their styles worlds apart, yet he liked her. More than liked, in fact, although he was fighting the urge to make it be anything else. He knew what worked for him, and quick and temporary wasn't it. Which meant they needed to stay on a professional level, he reminded himself, and made himself focus on her rundown of the lab results, which he'd been only halfway paying attention to.

One piece of information, though, had stuck out. "Hang on, back up. It's a genetically engineered organism?"

"It's looking that way, possibly a hybrid of a mushroom, an air plant and a sulfur bacterium at the very least."

"Why would you want to cross those together?"

She gave an eloquent shrug. "Your guess is as good as mine. The air plant allows it to live suspended. As for the others, we're looking at a toxic fungus and an anaerobe. It'll take more of an expert than me to figure out why you'd put those two together unless you wanted...I don't know, a long-lived poison, maybe?"

Jack stilled. "How about a drug that's addictive at low doses but deadly at higher doses?"

Excitement seared through him. Had they just found the source of the Death Stare?

Chapter Seven

"A drug?" Tori frowned, then shook her head. "I'm not an expert, but I'd tend to say that would be a long shot. A poison, sure. But the amatia isn't a 'shroom of the psychedelic variety." She thought back to a couple of snippets she'd overheard during his nightly base-touch with his boss. "Are you thinking of this Death Stare case?" At his clipped nod, she pressed, "Tell me about it." When he hesitated, she said, "I learned a long time ago not to discount even the most far-fetched-sounding idea. Occam's razor doesn't always apply when it comes to Mother Nature... or humankind."

His lips twitched. "The simplest explanation isn't always the right one?"

"Not in my experience. So, the Death Stare. Start talking." It wasn't just the case she was curious about either. Clearly this one was personal to him.

After a moment's hesitation, he said grimly, "Okay, the short version is that there have been fourteen deaths that we know of, probably more since it's mostly been hitting the kinds of people who don't check themselves into the ER when they start feeling crummy." He shrugged, but his expression didn't match the casual gesture. "Anyway, it's seriously nasty stuff. It's highly addictive, easy to OD on and the withdrawal is a killer. Literally. Worse, according to the lab results, it's not any one thing. It's this funky blend of a bunch of known drugs plus a couple of components nobody can quite figure out. The analysts are working on it, but meanwhile we're losing good men out there on the streets."

"Cops?" she asked, though she knew the parlance.

He nodded. "Three were shot the other day, trying to get a bead on the drug traffic. But cops aren't the only good guys out there. Sometimes a good guy is just a good guy."

"I know that," she said, surprised because she wasn't used to cops who knew it. In her experience, the protect-and-serve mentality came with a good dose of "us versus them." Then again, she was starting to get the sense that Jack wasn't like any of the other cops she'd known before.

He grimaced. "Yeah. Sorry. Touchy subject." When he paused, she just waited, having learned that it sometimes took him a moment. Sure enough, he eventually continued, "One of the ODs was a good friend of mine, Ray Prews. We knew each other all through school, hated each other through junior high and then after that glommed as friends, bonding freshman year over the horrors of chem class." His eyes softened, saddened. "He was the guy who had it all, you know? Honors student, football star, good family, pretty much his pick of colleges."

This time when he stopped, she said, "What happened?"

"It's an old enough story—he got hurt a little, took some painkillers to play through it and got hurt worse, right around the time the early predictions were being made for the NFL draft that year. More drugs, more playing and he wound up with major surgery, a permanent limp, no contract and a hell of a drug habit." His lips thinned. "He came home, and things got worse rather than better. He kept using no matter what his family and friends said or did. He lied, stole and sneaked around until finally his parents staged an intervention and shipped him off to a rehab facility they couldn't really afford. He lasted three days before he checked himself out and came back to the city. Got a job working as muscle for a third-rate party-promoter-slash-drug-dealer, rented a room at a crappy motel, and pretty much cut us all off. Family, friends, nothing. It was like we didn't exist anymore, when all we wanted to do was help."

With another of her friends, acquaintances or coworkers, she might have reached across the table and squeezed his hand in support. With him, because she wanted to too much, she didn't let herself make the move. Instead, she said cautiously, "You can't help an addict until he's ready to make a change."

He grimaced. "I know that now. Hell, I knew it back then, we all did. But it's one thing to hear the experts say it and another to live it. Anyway, he eventually got to that point on his own. He met a girl at one of the clubs. She wasn't perfect—hell, neither of them was—but she had a daughter, and he fell for both of them and started to turn things around. Got a steadier job doing maintenance at the club the girlfriend—Ginger—was working at, got an apartment. He even reached out a little to his family, was starting to put that back together. And then one morning he didn't come home." Voice flattening to an all-too-familiar cop tone that carried facts but not emotions, distancing him from the pain, he said, "Ginger called me, and I did some checking around. I was angry at him, disappointed, thinking he'd slipped and was hiding out until he sobered up. But he wasn't. He was in the morgue as a John Doe because after the Death Stare got him, the alley rats had gotten his wallet and ID, his shoes, jacket. Hell, they practically left him naked."

Tori knew the tone, but always before she'd only seen the flat affect behind it, the "just the facts, ma'am" that her father and brothers hid behind when the going got tough. Now, though, she saw pain behind the mask. "I'm sorry," she said softly.

"Not your fault."

But there was a piece of it that *was* her fault, if only obliquely. "I took you away from the investigation, didn't I?"

"No, *I* took me away from it," he said. "After Ray died, I threw myself into the case, and not in a good way. I worked it even on my downtime, let the other stuff in my life slide, got obsessed…and wound up making some mistakes. Most recently with a witness, a street guy named Hawk who said he saw the guy who sold the Death Stare to the vic. When I got there, though, he was all scared-looking, and said he couldn't remember anything. I leaned on him pretty hard. There was, uh, an incident, and my bosses decided they couldn't keep ignoring the problem any longer."

Dull shock twisted through her. "You beat him up because he wouldn't tell you what he saw?"

He shot her a reproachful look. "Try, I took a step toward him, he overreacted, slipped on some alley slime, fell and broke his wrist." He paused, then said quietly, "Do you really think I would have gone after someone like that?" More than his words, his tone of quiet entreaty reached into her and squeezed her heart.

She flushed. "I'm sorry. You haven't done anything to deserve that. It's just that I also know that grief and anger can make people do things they might not do otherwise. So maybe I, uh, jumped to a conclusion." More, she was checking baggage into the conversation, which wasn't her style.

He looked more resigned than offended, though. "Unfortunately, you're not the only one who looked at the equation of one obsessed cop plus one reluctant witness equals slip-and-fall injury, and assumed I'd gotten rough with him. Add in an eager junior partner at one of the local firms, looking to make his name with a big pro bono case, and you get a whole lot of trouble brewing. Which is what I got, along with an Internal Affairs investigation and some desk time." His face darkened with frustration. "The case is going to settle and the other stuff will go away—the only thing I'm guilty of is getting in the guy's face, after all—but in the meantime, I'm off the case right when the others need me the most."

"I'm sorry," she said, and again, would have touched his arm if he'd been someone else. "You had good intentions."

"Which doesn't get me anywhere if I'm not going by protocol." He exhaled. "Hell, they were right to bench me. I had lost perspective and was running on more heart than head. If it hadn't been Hawk getting hurt, it would have been something else, and that 'something else' might have been even more damaging to the department and the case." As he paused, his expression went faintly rueful. "Tucker told me to use the time out here in the backcountry to get my head screwed back on straight. Guess he was right after all."

"He seems like a smart guy."

"He's a good friend." He said it with the simple affection of a man who had many friends, which was yet another difference between them. He was surrounded by his close friends and family.

She lived among a sea of acquaintances. Even Chondra and June were convenient friends—not that she loved them any less, but she was self-aware enough, had been through it enough, to know that when she moved on to another lab, as she did every few years, they'd all make good faith efforts to keep in touch, but over time the friendships would fade. They always did.

Jack's friendships, though, were the sort that dated back forever. It was yet another example of how different they really were deep down inside.

Not wanting to look too closely at those differences just now, she filled the silence by asking, "What happened to Ray's girlfriend and her daughter?"

"A few of us helped them out right after, and are keeping an eye on them going forward, just making sure they're okay. It's what Ray would have wanted." He said it like that was nothing, as if anyone else would have done the same.

She knew different, though, and the knowledge squeezed a tight ache around her heart. He'd gone to war for a friend he'd lost touch with, and was stepping up now to make amends as if he owed something, even though he'd already done more than most people would have.

He was the kind of lawman the others in her life wanted to believe they were, she realized suddenly. Or maybe it wasn't all that sudden of a realization. Maybe she'd been sneaking up on the idea ever since that first harrowing ride down from the Forgotten, when he hadn't wasted time berating her or issuing a string of I-told-you-so's, but had just buckled down and got both of them out to safety. And then, based only on her conviction that the forest was in grave jeopardy, he had stayed with her, worked with her, even though part of him had to be dying to get back down to the city and pick up what he could of the Death Stare investigation. He hadn't put that on her, though; he'd kept it to himself until now.

He's the real deal, she thought, and felt nerves sizzle. Because if she'd felt a little out of her depth when she first met him, now she was totally treading water, caught in the countercurrent pulls of attraction versus her better sense. Without really meaning to, she said softly, "You're one of the good guys, aren't you, Jack?"

Heat kindled in his eyes. "I don't know about that, but I think I should give you fair warning. You don't want to say things like that—or look at me like you're doing right now—unless you mean it."

She hesitated, realizing suddenly that they were getting close to the point where they had to choose to either keep things professional, or go over the line to personal. And once they crossed the line, they could decide not to go any further, but there was no going back. "I'm not sure what I mean right now," she said finally. "You're nothing like I thought you were going to be." That wasn't quite professional, but it didn't take it all the way to personal either.

"What were you expecting?"

"Someone who thinks being a cop gives him enough karma points to make up for him being pushy—or worse, indifferent—in other areas of his life. Someone who thinks his own stuff is far more important than mine, because people matter more than trees, and cops matter more than civilians. Someone who—" Realizing that her heart was thudding too fast, her blood running too high, even though none of those sins belonged to him, she broke off and blew out a breath. "Sorry."

"Don't be. It explains a few things." He paused, leaving it hanging.

She hesitated because it just wasn't her style to talk about her family. As far as she was concerned, people should take her at face value without worrying how she had gotten that way. To her surprise, though, she found that she didn't mind the question coming from him, and might not even mind answering it. She trusted him enough, wanted him enough. And if he was ready to give a little, as hinted by his asking personal questions even though he knew there were fundamental places where they didn't mesh, relationship-wise, then she could give a little, too.

So, after taking a sip to wet her suddenly dry throat, she said, "My father is a cop, along with my sister and two of my three brothers. My youngest brother is an MP, which wasn't that much of a leap. It's the same way with the rest of my family—almost everybody does the protect-and-serve thing…or else is a housewife to a guy who does." In the interest of fairness, she added, "I'm not the only exception to that rule, granted, but it feels like I am sometimes, especially when they start in on the whole 'what we do is so much more important than what you do' routine."

He arched a brow, but didn't comment, just got up and started clearing the plates. She started to rise to help him, but he waved her back down and said, "So…I take it that means there aren't many cops among your exes?"

"Definitely no cops," she said quickly, but hesitated a beat before she said, "and not really any exes either. At least not the way I think you mean, the kind that break your heart and leave you raw after. I'm more of a 'get together, have some fun, move on' kind of girl." She said it breezily, but heat touched her cheeks. She wasn't offering, not exactly. But she was testing the waters, and they both knew it.

So was he, though, and he'd been the one to start the personal stuff. But the thing was, she wasn't sure whether they were trying to talk themselves into something or out of it.

When he didn't say anything, just went about rinsing off their dishes, she added, "It's another part of my being the black sheep of the family, you see. Not only did I skip going into law enforcement, but I also don't own a house, haven't ever been married or even really seriously involved with a guy and change universities every few years. My dad says it's a phase and my brothers and sister call it self-indulgent. They don't seem to get that I'm happy this way and, more, that I'd be miserable if I tried to shackle myself into a life like theirs. It works for them, great…but that doesn't mean it has to work for me."

They both knew she wasn't just talking about her family anymore.

"What about your mom?" he asked without turning around. "You haven't really mentioned her."

She was aware that his tone had shifted a little even though the difference was difficult to pinpoint over the rushing sound of water. She thought, though, that he'd put a distance between them that hadn't been there moments earlier.

We don't have to do this, she thought. She didn't say it, though, because they had already gone too far.

So, telling herself that she couldn't worry about whether he liked what he was hearing, she said, "If I haven't mentioned my mom, it's because there's zero friction there. She and I are flips of the same coin. At least we are these days. She and my dad got divorced right around the time I left home—they waited until I was out of the house. Or, rather, *she* waited. My dad would have gone on indefinitely the way they were, with him working and her keeping the house, and them taking their two weeks on the lake every summer, and nothing ever changing really. He didn't want to hear that she was feeling bored, stifled and *stuck,* still living in the same town, with the same streets, same stores, same people she'd known forever. He loved it, and thought that if she didn't love it, she just wasn't trying hard enough."

Aware that her voice had gone sharp, she blew out a breath and told herself to ease up. "Anyway, she's happier now with Cesare. They don't have a ton of money, but they still manage to travel the world together, picking up work as they go. She's even writing a series of magazine articles about their adventures. They'll start coming out next month."

She paused, waiting for a comment, a nod, anything. But he just stood there, pretending to dry a plate with a bright purple towel.

Mouth going dry, though she couldn't have said exactly what she was worried about—there wasn't anything between them, so there was nothing to lose, right?—she continued, "My dad remarried, too, and this time he picked a woman who likes his routine, likes sticking close to home and making it a nice place for him to come back to after work. My two older brothers both married nest builders, too. Which is a good thing because if either of them had fallen for a woman who wanted more than that, it would have been a disaster." She paused, aware that the air was suddenly strung tight with hurt and tension even though she didn't know why. "Are…are you okay?"

He said something under his breath, too low for her to hear. Then, moving slowly, deliberately, he racked the plate with a sharp click of stoneware on stoneware, wadded up the purple towel and tossed it on the counter and then turned toward her. His face was stern and set, that of a man who was ready to make an arrest, read rights, inform a family of a loved one's death. But again she saw the pain beneath the mask.

"Jack?" she said softly, finally rising and taking a step toward him, reaching to touch, to soothe.

"Don't." The word was a harsh rasp, his uplifted hand a signal to stay away. "I need…" He made a vague gesture toward the door. "I'm going to check the perimeter. Stay inside until I come back."

They both knew he'd checked it an hour earlier, and the lights on the console beside the door were green across the board.

She told herself to let it go, to let *him* go, but she was caught by the pain. "Look, I know we don't know each other and we're not really friends. Not the kind you have, anyway. But maybe that's not a bad thing right now…and I'm a good listener."

He started for the door, but then stopped and turned

back to meet her eyes. "I don't think this is a good idea." It wasn't the cop looking at her now, but the man. And the man wasn't just turning down her offer of a listening ear. He was turning it all down, turning *her* down.

She wasn't surprised that he'd make the smarter, safer call. She *was* a little surprised, though, how much it stung, driving a sliver of pain into her heart, one that said she'd been hoping it would go the other way even more than she'd realized. But she only said, "I'm sorry to hear that."

"Me, too." But he walked out anyway, closing the door firmly behind him.

She stared at the door long after his footsteps faded outside, not really sure what she was feeling. Or, rather, not sure which of the competing emotions was winning. She was frustrated by the churning warmth that never quite went away when he was in the vicinity and sorely disappointed that he'd turned down her not-quite-an-offer, yet at the same time, she felt for him, wanted to ease whatever hurt she'd just accidentally caused.

"Leave him alone," she told herself. "If he'd wanted to keep talking he wouldn't have walked away." But that wasn't entirely true either. If he was anything like her— and she was coming to realize that there were more similarities than differences, at least in some regards—he might just have needed to be outside breathing the night air and clearing his head. Once he did that, he might welcome the company out there under the stars.

"Don't push it," she told herself. "Go upstairs and get back to work."

She went after him instead.

Chapter Eight

Jack heard her footsteps on the stairs leading up to the observatory platform, and just shook his head.

Of course she hadn't stayed inside. And of course she had come after him. No doubt she saw him as akin to one of her sick forests: in need of tending, lest a catastrophic collapse follow. Or maybe she saw him as something more than that, something—or, rather, someone—she cared about within her own comfort zone of caring. Which would only complicate things more.

He shouldn't have let the conversation get so personal. *Let it?* he thought with an inner snort. Hell, he'd taken it there, pushing her to open up to him, no doubt with some deep-seated and arrogant belief that she was secretly tired of the traveling lifestyle and ready to settle down with the right man.

More, her comments about her brothers and father had struck a nerve because he'd been that guy. Hell, he *was* that guy. That was what had driven him out of the kitchen, and it was what had him now gripping the waist-high railing that edged the platform, and staring up into the night sky.

He'd killed the floodlights—only a mild security risk given that the other sensors were still online—and the moon was only a thin sliver behind him, leaving the night dark and gorgeous, and filled with far more stars than the city ever saw. The sky was gorgeous, endless. It made him feel small and insignificant, yet at the same time reminded him that he and Tori were far more similar than they were different.

But that was the thing, wasn't it? Sure, they had some things in common—more, it turned out, than he would have thought at first—but a couple of the things they differed on were deal breakers for him.

She stopped at the edge of the platform and stood there for a moment, watching him. He knew he should tell her to leave, that she would go if he asked and they would probably both be better off. They could go back to their unstated truce with the memory of that one kiss between them. At least he thought they could. Maybe that, too, was wishful thinking.

Instead of sending her away, though, he looked up into the sky, and said, "When I was a kid I used to dream about growing wings and flying up toward the stars. I don't remember the last time I thought about it—probably years. But I know for damn sure that tonight is the first time I've felt like flying in a long, long time."

"To get away from me?" Her footsteps were quiet on the sturdy observation platform, leaving him to sense her approach in the fine tingle of electricity that raced across his skin, making him dig his fingers into the railing so he wouldn't turn, touch, take.

"No, never," he said. That was the difference between them, wasn't it? She wanted to escape; he wanted to stay right where he was. "It wasn't ever about escaping. I've never wanted to be anyplace else." How could he? There, in the pitch blackness, he was aware of the backcountry spread out around them, falling away from the observatory. Even down in the city, where the starlight was dimmed, he knew the mountains were near, that his friends and family were there. The people he cared about, the ones he was sworn to protect.

"Not even now?"

He sighed. "Okay, maybe a little." He turned to face her, finding her to be little more than a darker shape in the shadows, with a gleam of starlight coating her face and giving her depth and substance.

She linked her hands together in front of her body, the action more a whisper of sound than motion, and said, "I told myself to go upstairs and leave you alone."

He felt his lips curve. "How did that work out for you?"

"Not so well. But I'm not staying. I just wanted to say…" She paused as if choosing her words carefully. "You don't owe me anything, Jack. If anything, I owe you for helping me out the way you have over the past few days, despite the fact that you would have rather been working on the drug case. I know you'll say you were just doing your job, but it's been more than that to me. And…well, anyway, I just wanted you to know that I'm grateful for that, and I'm not asking for more, or expecting it, or anything. And I'm sorry if I went too far just now, and I hope you'll keep in mind that the lifestyle that works for me doesn't work for most other people, and vice versa. Just because I don't want to put down roots and settle in, that doesn't mean it's the wrong answer for you."

He hesitated, then admitted, "That's pretty much what Kayla said, too." Until he said the name, he hadn't been certain he was going to go there. It felt like stepping over a line he hadn't realized was there until a few minutes ago, when Tori had been talking about her brothers and it had started feeling like she was talking about him. He'd heard all the same arguments, after all, only in another woman's voice. "You didn't do or say anything wrong, Tori. You just hit a nerve, that's all."

"Kayla." She repeated the name. "Ex-wife?"

"Ex-fiancée." It seemed like too simple a word for what she had been to him, though, prompting him to say, "I knew her most of my life, though. We knew each other as kids, went steady in high school, did the long-distance thing when she went away to college and I stayed local… and then she moved back so we could be together when I went into the academy. I asked her to marry me right after graduation, when I started out as a uniform, and she said yes. We knew we were young, but we figured we would keep growing up in the same direction. At least I did."

He paused, and then when she didn't say anything, shrugged and continued, "Anyway, she wanted to be in TV news, but took a magazine job instead, so she could stay local and still move forward. But then, when we were planning the wedding, a big station in Chicago offered this dream internship. So we postponed things for six months while she did the internship. Then another year when she got offered a job…and, well, we eventually sort of slid into a vague promise of 'we'll plan it when things settle down.' Only they didn't. Or, rather, she didn't. She just kept orbiting farther and farther away…until eventually she stopped coming back."

He sighed. "She said I was stifling her, that Bear Claw was stifling her, that she needed to leave because she loved herself, not because she didn't love me. And she said lots of the same things you were saying about your father and your brothers... So, yeah, it stung."

"Because you still miss her or because you hadn't really looked at it from her—or, rather my—perspective before?"

He exhaled a long, slow breath. "Wow." He didn't think he'd been looking for sympathy, or for Tori to apologize on Kayla's behalf or anything like that, but the sudden burn of irritation said otherwise. Filling his lungs, he concentrated on smoothing out the suddenly raw edges even though he knew they colored his voice when he said, "Maybe we should call it a night after all."

"You're probably right." She sounded equally annoyed, but then sighed out a long breath and said, voice softer, "I'm sorry."

"For the delivery, but not the content?"

Her headshake showed in the wan starlight. "I shouldn't have come up here. I guess I thought... I don't know. That maybe I could help you somehow, pay you back for helping me these past few days. Instead, I just made it worse."

"Maybe we needed to do this," he said, wondering if the heat would die down now, as his subconscious—and his libido—had come to grips with the fact that she wasn't even close to the right woman for him to be involved with. "Maybe we needed to get to this point, where it's glaringly obvious that we might be attracted to each other but we're coming at this from two totally different places. You don't do serious and I'm not wired for casual...which doesn't leave us with any middle ground."

"Maybe. But at the risk of making things even worse, let me ask you something." She took a couple of steps and closed the gap between them. "If you really loved Kayla, why wouldn't you go out on the road with her? Shouldn't being with the person you love be more important than just a place?"

He'd heard that one before, too, and could answer without heat: "Home and family are more than a place for me, Tori, and my career is more than a job. Any woman who'd expect me to give up any of those things doesn't know me nearly well enough to ask."

He expected an argument, was braced for it. He wasn't prepared for her to take the two more small steps needed to bring her inside his space, though, and he wasn't braced for her to grab his collar and use it to tug his face down to her level. But that was what she did.

They stood there for a breathless moment, nose-to-nose in the darkness. Then she leaned in, so her breath was warm against his lips as she whispered, "News flash, Detective. I'm not asking you to give up anything except your three-date, five-date, ten-date rules. And I'm offering fireworks in return."

Heat flared through him, lit him up and hollowed him out. As his senses started to churn, he told himself to back off, back away, call it a night. Instead, as the scent and feel of her burned in his blood and branded itself deep in his psyche, he caught the back of her neck.

And he moved in.

They met halfway in a kiss that instantly heated, becoming far more than the simple press of lips and touch of tongues, turning instead to urgent desire. The clutch of her hands at the back of his neck said *Come closer.* The hum at the back of her throat said *Yes, there.* And the slide of her tongue said *More.*

So he went closer, touched there, gave more and, there in the concealing darkness, with them the only people around for miles and miles, he gave in to what his body wanted, what the heat demanded. He gathered her close and leaned back against the railing, and was suddenly very aware of the free fall that waited behind him, seeming to beckon for them both. But there was no reason to take the plunge when everything he wanted right then was in his arms, kissing him back with fervent abandon.

She was warm and womanly, and where in the daylight her personality made her seem larger than her physical self, in the darkness her unabashed sensuality seemed to exceed her physical form, making her seem to be everywhere at once, surrounding him with light touches and inciting caresses that made his blood burn and his heartbeat thunder in his ears. She tempted him with her mouth, seduced him with touches that trailed across his ribs and down his flanks to hidden spots that made him shudder against her and groan into their heated kiss.

Moaning, she swayed against him, fisting her hands in his shirt and hanging on as if she'd lost her balance. His equilibrium was long gone, swept away by the flames that raged within him, blazing hotter and faster than drought-spawned wildfires as he filled his hands with her hips and cupped the sweet curves of her bottom. Lifting, he drew her up against his body, let her feel him hard and wanting behind his zipper.

Her breasts pressed against his chest, inciting him with the hint of hard, budded nipples beneath her shirt and bra. He wanted to cup them, touch them, rub them until she moaned into his mouth. His pulse thudded as he lowered her to her feet, following her mouth so their lips never parted, so the kiss never ended, but instead continued on in a swirl of flavor, sensation and intimate heat while he tugged her shirt out of her waistband and slipped his hands beneath.

Her skin was so soft it felt like a dream—warm, fluid and yielding—and she purred against his mouth, wordlessly urging him onward. He slid his hands up from the slight flare of her hips to the lean dip of her waist, and then higher so he could skim the heels of his hands along the edges of her breasts. Lace brushed softly against his skin, achingly feminine. He traced the contours of her bra and then, when she arched into his touch, cupped her fully, cradling her erect nipples in the crooks of his thumbs so he could rub, gently at first and then with increasing pressure as she moaned her pleasure.

Lust stampeded through him and their kiss went wetter, turning carnal. He was dying to strip her naked, wanted to be naked himself, skin on skin, so he could kiss every inch of her, lick his way into her secret moistness, and—

Jack froze as the rules—and the mistakes that had helped him craft them—came crashing in on him. His eyes flew open and he stilled within the kiss, withdrawing his tongue but not breaking the connection of their lips.

Oh, holy hell. What was he doing? This wasn't date ten, wasn't date three. It wasn't even a date. It was… Damn it, he didn't know what it was, except that this wasn't him. It wasn't the way he did things, wasn't the way he wanted to live his life.

He didn't know when or if she opened her eyes, didn't know what she was thinking or feeling; he knew only that his hands were on her breasts, her taste in his mouth and things had gone way too far for his peace of mind.

Although she must have felt the tension in his body, her lips curved against his and lingered for a soft, chaste kiss before she drew away, and there was a husky, aroused rasp in her voice when she said, "See what I mean, Detective? Fireworks."

Yeah. There was no question about that.

Clearing his throat, he dropped his hands from her breasts to her hips, where he smoothed down her shirt for a moment, knowing he had to let go, but not quite ready to stop touching her. Needing to, though, he pushed away from the railing, bringing their bodies once more flush before he took a big step back, away from her.

The night air was very cool on his body, chilling the places that were warm from her touch. "That was... Wow."

She laughed. "I'll take that and send it back in your direction because it was 'wow' for me, too." She paused, and there was a new, more searching note in her voice as she said, "So, what do you say? Just a few days, no harm, no foul, all fun, completely off the books and only when we're safely inside the perimeter here, so you don't need to be watching either of our backs. Come on...what can it hurt?"

But that was the thing, wasn't it? Because going into something knowing it was temporary didn't necessarily stop it from hurting.

"I can't." He almost looked around to see who had said that, but he didn't because he knew the words had come from him. And he knew they were the right ones, no matter how much it sucked to turn her down. "I'm sorry, but I just can't do it, not like this. You're amazing. But this...it isn't me."

There was a weighty pause before she said, "Is it because of the job? Because you're protecting me?"

"No, I'm protecting me, and it doesn't have anything

to do with the job. I…I just don't do casual, Tori. I'm not wired that way. The couple of times I've tried to keep it light, I've gotten in too deep anyway. And with those ladies, I didn't start out feeling half of what I'm feeling right now."

"We could…" She trailed off, though, and sighed. "Well, damn."

"Exactly. We can make all the inner promises we want, but whatever's between us, whatever that was just now, it's not something we're going to be able to negotiate with. I don't know about you, but just now I wasn't thinking about anything but what I wanted to do to you, what I wanted us to do together." Even saying it like that brought new heat thudding in his veins.

In the starlight, he could barely make out the curve of lips gone moist and full with their kisses. "When you put it that way, it's hard to be offended."

"Don't be. Please."

"I'm not. Really, I'm not. Disappointed, yes. Turned on and looking at a long, restless night? Definitely. But I've got a relationship rule of my own, and it's called 'no harm, no foul.' I'm a big girl. I can take a 'no, thank you,' especially when it's delivered like this one was, and for solid reasons that the scientist in me can't even begin to argue with." She moved into his space again, got him by the collar and tugged him down.

He thought about resisting but didn't have it in him. His body yielded to her and he lowered his face to hers as his heart thudded softly in his chest.

She kissed him on the cheek. "Good night, Jack."

It was an effort of will not to turn his lips to hers, not to reach for her and hang on tight. Instead, he said, "Goodnight, Tori. And thanks for everything."

"Everything?"

"Having dinner with me. Pushing me to talk about Kayla a little…and the rest of it."

She sighed softly, gave his collar one last tug and then let him go and stepped away. "Don't stay out here forever brooding, okay? I want to get an early start tomorrow."

"Yeah, okay." Turning back to the railing, he braced his forearms and stared out into the night as he listened to her footsteps fade down the stairwell, then go muted on the packed dirt. Moments later, the door to the main house opened and closed, leaving him alone in the darkness.

He stayed there for a long, long time. Long enough, even, to convince himself that if he squinted, he could almost see the lights of Bear Claw City. Home.

For a change, the thought didn't make him feel any better.

"I THOUGHT YOU SAID you'd get rid of the scientist and her cop." The edge in the Investor's voice sent an unpleasant jolt through Percy, one that said *You're in trouble.*

Granted, he'd been in trouble almost since the beginning when the voters upgraded him from acting mayor to mayor and he'd celebrated with a far-too-expensive weekend in Vegas that he'd used city money to cover. Couple that with a get-rich-quick promise from an old friend that had turned out to be a Ponzi scheme and a couple of other dips into the till, and he'd been tap-dancing to hide the embezzlement behind Bear Claw's financial woes for years now. He'd become an expert at making things disappear from one place and reappear in another, at least until the whole al-Jihad terrorism scare had put the city under some serious federal scrutiny. Then, he'd needed to repay the money, and do it fast.

Thus, the Investor.

Now, though, as Percy looked around his office at city hall—at the glossy wood and stacked library shelves, the acre of polished desk, the fleet of sleek computers and the wall of photos of him mugging with a select handful of celebs who came through Bear Claw each year—he wished he'd told the Investor to take a hike when he'd gotten that first phone call. He would have found another way. He always had before.

At the time, though, the offer had seemed like the answer to his prayers—money in exchange for access to the Forgotten. A real estate transaction, nothing more. But when that had gone sour and the voice on the phone had started asking for more and more, things had started rolling downhill, accelerating fast. These days, he was asking for the impossible.

"I did what I could." Percy kept his voice level. *Don't let him know you're afraid.*

"They were out at the old campsite again today."

"Not officially."

"I don't give a crap whether it's an official investigation or not!" The Investor's voice cracked down the line. "You said you'd get them out of the damn forest!"

"Like I said, I did what I could," Percy insisted, darting a look at his office door, even though he'd closed and locked it himself. "It's not like I can call over to the cops and have Williams ordered down off the mountain. He's on leave. And besides, it'd look suspicious."

"It'll look a damn sight more suspicious when I leak your real financials to the media."

A prickle of greasy sweat itched along Percy's spine. "You wouldn't dare. You need me."

"I'll make do without you if it becomes necessary." The Investor paused. When the mayor didn't say anything, satisfaction smoothed his tone back to something approaching normal as he said, "Deal with them. I don't care how, just get it done. But make sure it looks like an accident because I can't afford to have the militia rumors resurfacing. Which means *you* can't afford to have it happen either. Understand?"

"I…" Percy swallowed queasily. "I understand. I'll take care of them."

Somehow.

Chapter Nine

The next morning, Jack and Tori got up early and headed for the Forgotten with little more than "Coffee?" and "God, yeah" between them.

As the miles rolled beneath the SUV's tires, Tori thought that the silence in the cab wasn't strained so much as pensive. She didn't try to guess at his thoughts—she didn't dare—but she was very aware that there had been none of his usual sidelong looks…and equally aware that she missed them.

Let it go, she told herself for the twentieth time. They'd each said their pieces the night before, and their passionate make-out session hadn't changed anything really, except to make it that much more difficult to sit a few feet away from him and not glance over at the long lines of his jean-clad thighs as he jockeyed the heavy vehicle along the narrow track, or admire the ropy lines of his tanned forearms, which were bared beneath the rolled-back sleeves of his forest-green button-down.

So, deciding she didn't have to deny herself the scenery, even if it was look-don't-touch territory, she let herself glance, let herself admire. And she let herself wish things had gone differently.

They hadn't, though, and she couldn't say he'd made

the wrong call. Granted, after tossing and turning her way through exactly the sort of long and restless night she had predicted, she couldn't say much of anything except that she was tired, her reserves were low and her emotions were way too close to the surface. All of which together warned her that it was time to move on, albeit earlier than she had planned.

In reality, she had plenty of samples. She needed access to a fast, reliable internet connection so she could look into the three organisms that appeared to be related to the Bear Claw fungus, and see if there were any ways to counter those progenitors. Not to mention that if the Bear Claw infection proved to be genetically modified, she would need to report it to the proper authorities. Given the speed of the spread, she intended to keep working on a cure, but she didn't need to be on-site to do the work. If anything, she was slowing herself down at this point.

And, yeah, that was the opposite of the logic she had used with Chondra last night. She could admit that, at least inwardly, and move on from it.

As the SUV tilted upward once more, entering the last long upgrade that segued into the narrow switchback road to the deserted militia campground, she turned in the passenger seat, shifting to face him and start the conversation that began, "I think it's time for me to head back to the university." The fact that she hesitated, knowing how he would see the situation, was added evidence that it was time to leave. She didn't let anyone—not her bosses or her coworkers, never mind her lovers or friends—make her feel awkward about the way she lived her life, and she didn't intend to start now.

So stop stalling, she told herself, a little amused to realize she was doing it. A little unnerved, too. "Hey, listen," she began, "I think—"

"Did you see that?" He eased up on the gas and leaned out the driver's window to look up. "Sorry," he said from out there, his words carrying back to her over the engine noise. "I didn't mean to interrupt."

"What did you see?" she asked, pitifully willing to be diverted.

"An eagle, I think."

"A barred eagle?" The not-quite-extinct birds were prominently marked with black-and-white stripes against a mottled brown background. She craned to follow his line of sight. "I haven't seen one yet."

Although the birds had been spotted in and around the infection site, they had proven far more elusive than she would have expected, given how often they had been noted in the area right after the militia's discovery. The hint of a connection stirred in her brain, there and gone so quickly that she didn't get a chance to grab on to the thought. Not when she was scanning the sky, trying to see the distinctive five-fingered wingspread of a raptor while hanging on to the door handle as Jack sent the SUV into the first of the switchbacks.

"It disappeared beyond that ridge." He had his eyes back on the road now, but gestured to a low series of rocky hills nearly hidden beneath the green fur of healthy trees that hadn't yet been hammered by the infection. And wouldn't be, if she had anything to say about it.

Thinking about the case was a welcome relief in one respect but a major frustration in another: she wasn't making enough progress and she was running out of time.

An ecosystem is like a rocky wall poised to collapse in

a massive avalanche, she remembered one of her professors routinely saying, *take out any one type of rock and the whole thing falls apart.* The Forgotten was an important ecosystem, not just because of the effect an outbreak could have on Bear Claw Canyon, but because it was home to the only known wild population of barred eagles, which had long been thought extinct, killed by heavy metal poisoning because they preferred to nest near…

"Copper!" she said, straightening suddenly as it clicked into place.

He glanced over and their eyes met for the first time that morning. "What about it?"

"The eagles died off because they liked to nest near the old copper mines, right? Well, we've been trying to figure out why the eagles, the fungus and the militia all happened to show up in the same place at the same time. What if the connection is the copper?"

Jack considered it as he swung the SUV along the last of the narrow reversals on the uphill before they crowned the low mountain and started the treacherous downward trail. "There's never been any evidence of copper deposits—or any real natural resource up in the Forgotten. That's one of the main reasons nobody ever tried to do anything with the land."

"Maybe we're not talking about a deposit. Maybe it's more diffuse than that, sort of a copper leech field that neither the old-time prospectors nor the newer technologies would consider viable for mining purposes."

"But then why—" He broke off, expression clearing. "The engineered fungus. You think it's using the trees to pull the metal up out of the soil? Is that even possible?"

"There are stranger things on heaven and earth, Detective." Excitement hummed through her now as the connections started lining up. "That explains the eagles, or at least it starts to. Either they've been hiding up in the Forgotten all this time, attracted to the diffuse copper deposits, or a remnant population was hiding somewhere else coppery and was drawn to the Forgotten once the fungal infection took hold and started concentrating the metal."

"You're sure the fungus is new? Oh, right," he said, answering his own point. "It's man-made. Of course it's new."

"Exactly. The DNA technology we're talking about is cutting-edge. Not the splicing and stuff—that's pretty old-school. But it would have taken some serious knowledge of all three organisms—the bacterium, the fungus and the air plant—to integrate them into a whole new species built for this specific purpose. A whole bunch of labs—including the one I did my thesis work in—are doing similar work to create living biological sensors and scrubbers designed to detect and clean up industrial pollution in rivers and lakes. That's mostly on the bacterial side of things, though. This is taking it up to a whole new level."

"Any idea who would be capable of doing the work?"

"Chondra's putting out feelers. I'll have a list of names for you by the end of the day."

The road flattened out at the crest of the high hill, and for a moment, most of the Forgotten was spread out in front of them in a gorgeous vista that today, as every other day for the past three, made her catch her breath in awe.

The dusty road winding downhill, with a rubble-strewn cliff face on one side and a sheer, guardrail-free drop on the other, was a golden ribbon separating the rocky barrens of the mountaintop from the vibrant green forest ecosystems below. In the near distance, another ribbon—this one a deeper, richer bronze punctuated with an occasional glint of gold where the sunlight gleamed off the mud-browned water—snaked among stands of trees that had darker leaves that were hazed with the white of infection, along with the strange patches that indicated where the fungus had died off and the trees had become reinfected. Again, a connection niggled at her brain. This time, though, it refused to come clear.

She sighed. "It really is beautiful out here."

"That it is," he said without looking at her. As he let the SUV start down the winding descent, careful to keep the wheels in the hardened ruts, he added, "Please tell me that whoever you've got asking questions is being careful. Because if you're right about all this being connected, those questions could get back to the wrong people."

It was a good point, she acknowledged with a shimmer of dread. If she was on the right track with the copper, they might be dealing with more than just a lab trying to cover up the escape of a bioengineered organism, but rather its intentional release. "If the militia's left the Forbidden, though…"

"They might be looking for another place to set up operations, and won't be too happy about having scientists poking into their business."

The drought-baked roadway threatened to crumble a little, causing the vehicle to wallow closer to the edge. She clutched at the door handle and sent up a little prayer, but he navigated the treacherous section with the same cool competence he'd shown during their other trips. Once they were past the dangerous section, she said, "Chondra knows that this situation has the potential to get volatile, and is smart enough to keep her head down."

He nodded. But after a moment, he said, "What I don't get is, why are they bothering? Copper isn't particularly valuable, and there have to be easier ways to get it. Is there something special about the way the fungus uses it? Maybe it changes the metal somehow?"

"Beats me. That info is going to have to come from better biochemists than I. My job isn't to come up with the motive, it's to figure out how to save your forest."

"Amen," he said, and where a few days ago she might have thought he was mocking her, she knew him well enough now to know he was entirely serious. He might be a city boy, but he was at least partly a mountain man at heart.

And she shouldn't be thinking about his heart—or anything else beyond his bodyguarding skills, for that matter. They had been there, done that, made the decision.

His thoughts must have paralleled hers at least partway, though, because he suddenly said, "Listen, Tori. About last night."

Her stomach jumped and heat bloomed on her skin, but she didn't let herself think he wanted anything more than a rehash, or maybe to apologize even though he had nothing to be sorry for. She looked out her side window, where the glory of the Forgotten formed a backdrop for the reflection-shadow of her face, and said, "Let's just stick to the case, okay? Besides, I think we've said what we needed to say…unless you've got something new to add?"

He exhaled. "No, but—"

"Then let's leave it alone." Where last night at dinner she hadn't been able to reach out to him, somehow now she could stretch an arm across the wide console that separated them, and grip his shoulder briefly in a one-handed hug. "You're a good man, Detective. There's no blame here."

"Yeah, that's part of what's making it so hard." When she withdrew her hand, he let go of his double-fisted grip on the steering wheel to catch her fingers in his for a moment. "Look, I can't do things in fast-forward. I'm just not wired that way. But when this is over, if I asked you to stay for a while—"

"I wouldn't," she said quickly, not sure if the sudden spurt of heat was from flattery or fear. "I couldn't." She tugged her hand away, locked her fingers together in her lap, and stared blankly out the window at a small flock of birds flying below them, in the empty air beyond the cliff. "If I—" she began, but then broke off.

"If you what?"

She hadn't even been aware of the desire until she started to ask the question and choked on the implications. But there it was suddenly, front and center in her mind, and although she told herself not to bother, that she already knew what the answer would be, she couldn't *not* ask. "When this is over, if I asked you to come visit me for a while, would you…"

He blew out a breath and then slowly shook his head. "Probably not."

"Yeah, figured as much." She smiled sadly at her own reflection in the glass. Beyond the edge, the birds had angled down and were dropping together like an airplane squadron, headed for a section of white-tinged forest beneath the cliff. "I'm going to miss this place." *And you,* she thought but didn't say because what was the point.

She'd be leaving tomorrow, though she suddenly remembered that she hadn't actually told him that part. She had been about to, when he'd interrupted her to point out the… *Oh, wow!* She gaped out the window as the reality connected in her brain. The squadron she'd been watching wasn't just made of random birds; its members had barred wings and tails, mottled brown bodies and glided on wings that spread out at the ends like five-fingered hands. Those were barred eagles!

The environmentalist in her rejoiced at the sight of so many of the rare birds at one time, while her inner investigator noted that eagles weren't flocking birds by any stretch of the imagination. So why were they clustering together now?

"Stop!" she said quickly, reaching over to grab Jack's forearm in her excitement as she pointed. "Look!"

He followed her gesture and his eyes widened. "No kidding. Okay, hang on. Just let me get us to a good stopping place—" He twisted the wheel and pumped the brakes. "And we'll take a—" With zero warning, the brake pedal went suddenly to the floor and the steering wheel spun without turning the SUV one iota. "No!"

They had lost their steering and brakes!

Eagles forgotten in an instant of pure terror, Tori grabbed the door handle like a lifeline. She thought about jumping, but the cliff was too close on her side, the edge too close on his. They were trapped! Heart leaping into her throat, she managed a strangled gasp of *"Jack."*

The SUV was picking up speed, its tires bumping along in the ruts they had been following, but that wouldn't last long, because less than a half mile away, the road curved back around to the left and disappeared. Beyond the curve, a short section of beaten sand continued on straight, then ended, it seemed, in midair.

He cursed viciously and pumped the pedal, then went for the emergency brake and cursed again. Then he shouted, "Hang on!" Grabbing the shift lever, he wrenched the transmission into the lowest driving gear. Something slammed ominously inside the engine and the SUV shuddered and bucked, but the vehicle slowed measurably.

Her heart leaped. "It's working!"

"Don't count your eagles," he said through gritted teeth, shifting his grip on the gear lever, "until…they're…" He yanked the lever into the Park position. *"Hatched!"*

A second later, a louder slamming noise drowned him out and was followed by a metal-on-metal grating sound that made her cringe, but the SUV slowed even more. For a second she nearly cheered, thinking that he'd done it, he'd saved them. But then, horribly, the SUV bumped up out of the ruts and slewed sideways, skidding and churning up gravel as it kept going under its own momentum, heading for the curve in the road and the drop-off beyond.

Her breath rattled in her lungs. They weren't going to make it. They were going to go over the edge and—

Fingers grabbed her hand and dug in with a pressure so intense that it was almost painful, bringing her out of her sudden shocked numbness. She yanked her eyes up to Jack's, and saw his determination as he popped her belt and then his own, and then dragged her toward him.

That was when she saw his door hanging open, saw the dirt and gravel whipping past. "Oh, God." The words bled between her lips, dying as her lungs seized up. *I can't,* she thought wildly, *I—*

"Come on! We've got to jump!" And somehow the dotermination in his eyes got her heart pumping and her brain working once more. *Hurry. Hurry!* She fought to make her arms and legs work so she could scramble across and crouch awkwardly with him, terrifyingly aware that it was almost too late; they were practically on top of the edge. "Go!"

He launched himself away from the SUV, pulling her with him. They landed hard, with her partially on top of him, but still gravel bit into her shoulder and upper arm as inertia slid them toward the edge.

"No!" She screamed and dug in her boots, but to no avail.

He shouted and moved convulsively against her, and suddenly they weren't sliding anymore. They were stopped. Still. *Oh, God.* She didn't question how or why, couldn't do anything right then but cling to him and watch with utter horror as the back corner of his SUV went over the edge and suddenly tilted down.

"No." This time the word was more of a sob, one that burned her throat and eyes as the vehicle's dust-coated undercarriage popped into view for a second before the other far corner went over, and the gritty ledge crumbled with a sound that was almost like a sigh. Then the big car rolled and disappeared. Almost immediately, a rending, tearing, crashing noise rose up from down below.

And then… There was a moment of utter silence that seemed somehow out of place.

There was no movie explosion, no dramatic music, no nothing except a couple of pings of trickling dirt and Tori's dawning realization that they were in serious trouble. She lay limply against Jack, clutching his shirt and waistband and staring after the SUV in utter stunned shock. "It's gone," she said hollowly, knowing it was stupid even as she said it, but unable to come up with anything better.

He took a big, shuddering breath and then let it out on a single word. "Yeah." Then he shifted beneath her, making her realize just how much of him was cushioning the majority of her body, protecting her from the impact and the cutting gravel. Her scrapes were minor, the pain already starting to fade. But what about him?

Hands starting to shake now with reaction, she fumbled to roll off him. It wasn't until he sat up, flexing his hand with a grimace of pain, that she saw the matte black handle sticking out of the packed earth behind them and realized that he hadn't just gotten them out of the skidding SUV safely, but he'd also used his knife as a makeshift piton to stop their deadly slide. The shakes moved inward from her hands to her core, so her whole body shook as she realized just how much he'd done for her in the space of a few minutes, maybe less.

She had survived mudslides, rockslides, snakes, predators, faulty equipment and a multitude of the other dangers that came with the nature of her work. Never before, though, had she come so close to dying. Or, rather, being murdered. Because there was no way the steering and brakes failed together like that unless they'd been sabotaged.

The members of the Shadow Militia were still in the area…and they had tried to kill her and Jack to halt the investigation.

The knowledge took root and dug in, chilling her blood and making her shake harder. She had to believe that fall would have been fatal, if not instantly, then soon enough if they had been injured and unable to help themselves. They were far from civilization, far from help, cut off from

backup. Her breathing thinned even further at the list...
And at the knowledge that Jack had saved her life. Again.

"Hey," he rasped. "It's okay. You're okay." He paused,
eyes darkening. "You *are* okay, right?"

She nodded, panting as she stared around them and a
new, horrible thought occurred. "Are they out there? Are
they coming for us?" Suddenly the rugged vista that had
been hauntingly beautiful before now turned ominous and
terrifying.

He didn't insult her with platitudes. "I doubt it. If they
were going to follow us they wouldn't have bothered rig-
ging the SUV. They would have hit us with a rocket-
propelled grenade instead. Or if they wanted it to look
like an accident, they could have waited for us to drive up
and then dropped an avalanche on us." He shook his head.
"No, this smacks of someone who wanted to be far away
from the scene of the crime."

The matter-of-fact way he said it should have terrified
her further. Oddly, though, it steadied her a little, as did
the sight of him, big and capable-looking as he glanced
over to where the SUV had gone, and grimaced.

In fact, she couldn't take her eyes off him.

His shirt was torn at the shoulder and elbow, his pants
were smudged with dirt. He wasn't wearing his guns or
hat, and their absence reminded her that their supplies had
gone over the cliff. His badge still rode low on his belt,
though, and his eyes were the same cool mountain-lake
blue she had first noticed at the airport.

Her eyes filled, her heart lodged in her throat, and she
whispered, "Oh, God. Jack."

She didn't know which one of them moved first; all she
knew was that one second she was staring at him, stunned

by the knowledge that she owed him her life, and the next, she was in his arms.

And. It. Felt. Wonderful.

He surrounded her, curving his big body into and around her and banding his arms across her hips and shoulders as he dug in and just simply *held* her. She clung to him fiercely in return, still shaking as she twined her arms around his neck and pressed her cheek to his.

There was no kissing this time, no caressing, nothing but the basic human need for physical contact, the warmth and pressure of body against body that said *We're alive*.

"Thank you," she said against his neck. "Thank you, thank you, thank you."

He let her cling—and, she thought, clung a little in return—while her shakes subsided. Then, with a final squeeze, he eased away, though he kept a hand on her arm as if in reassurance that he wasn't going anywhere without her.

Tipping his head toward the edge of the broken-off ledge, he said, "Let's see if we can get to the wreck safely. The more gear we can get out of there, the more comfortable we're going to be until help arrives."

She blinked at him, sudden and unexpected hope kindling. "You got a distress signal out?"

"No, but if I don't check in tonight, Tucker will send out a search party first thing in the morning. We're right off the road, so we shouldn't be hard to find."

"Which means it'll be equally easy for whoever sabotaged the brake and steering lines to find us if they come looking to confirm the kill." She made herself say it, and felt the dread congeal in a hard knot in her stomach.

He nodded, not insulting her by trying to coddle.

"That's possible, which is why we're going to find a good, defensible position and do our damnedest to disappear. If, as it looks right now, the militia has been up here for months harvesting fungus, or copper, or whatever, and we couldn't find them even with the best high-tech the feds were able to get their hands on…well, I'm betting that we can stay invisible for one night, especially if we can reach the wreck and get our hands on some of that survival gear we've been hauling around."

She had no doubt he would get the equipment, even if it meant risking his own life to do so. But that wasn't what had her frowning and saying, "I think… I don't know."

Until his fingers tightened on hers, she hadn't realized he was holding her hand. "Trust me," he said, keeping his eyes steady on hers. "We're going to make it through this and get back down to Bear Claw safely."

"I do trust you." Instead of pulling away from him, she turned her palm and twined her fingers through his for a more intimate squeeze she probably wouldn't have gone for under any other circumstance. "I do… There's something else, though. A connection I'm missing. But I don't know…" She trailed off as motion caught her peripheral vision—a flash of mottled brown with a hint of black-and-white stripes. Whipping her head around, she focused on the eagles. There were three of them this time, winging together in the same direction as the last group.

He followed her gaze. "Huh. I think we've seen more of them in the last half hour than I've heard about in the past month."

"That's it!" She gaped as it came together suddenly inside her. "That's the connection! The eagles aren't just attracted to the fungus, they're attracted to whatever harvesting technique is being used to process it—and I'm betting there hasn't been any processing recently, or else it's been happening somewhere off-site. That's why nobody's seen them for a while. There wasn't any reason for them to congregate because there was no copper to lure them in!"

"You... Wow." He followed the eagles' flight path, expression pensive. After a moment, though, he nodded almost reluctantly. "You're right. It fits."

"What's more, if I'm right, then the eagles are telling us that whatever the militia is up to, they're doing it right now."

His eyes snapped back to hers. "Please tell me you're not thinking what I think you're thinking." When she didn't say anything right away, just looked at him solemnly, he groaned. "You *are* thinking it, aren't you?"

She didn't want to be thinking it, but yeah, she was. Her better sense might be clamoring for her to hide with him in some cave until tomorrow, as far off the radar as they could get. But her training and determination—and, damn it, the protect-and-serve motivation that was lodged in her DNA whether she liked it or not—said that she needed to do this and she needed to do it now, before their enemy realized that the sabotage had failed, and took even more drastic measures.

So she took a deep breath and shoved aside the fear, knowing that he was the only reason that was possible right now. She trusted him to have her back, and knew he would do the right thing. And this, whether they liked it, was the right thing. "We need to get in there, Jack, and we need to understand what they're doing to the Forgotten, and why." She paused, silently urging him to believe her, to believe *in* her. "So...what do you say? Want to see where those birds are headed?"

Chapter Ten

An hour later, as Jack hauled himself up another rocky ridge, cursing when his boots slipped in the loose shale and a couple of pulled muscles ached in protest, he still couldn't believe he'd let Tori talk him into hiking after the eagles.

They should have had their camp set up, with their exit routes scouted and their secure perimeter set up, leaving them to hunker down together and wait for rescue. Instead, they had recovered the survival gear—which, fortunately, had been banged up but salvageable, though the SUV was a write-off—stashed the bulk of the supplies in a deep, rocky niche near the crash site, and set off hiking roughly east-northeast along the beeline the birds seemed to be making.

She had put up a good argument, though, and when it came down to it, there was something to be said for their staying on the move rather than right near the SUV when there was a chance that their enemies would go looking for the wreck. Granted, they were headed into the hot zone rather than out of it, but she had promised this was just recon. No matter what they found, she would leave it to the pros to make a plan.

And, yeah, as they started down the ridge and the

white-hung trees closed around them once more, darkening the day and tainting the air with what he now recognized as the bloodlike tang of copper, he was willing to admit that maybe part of why he'd agreed without too much of a fight was because he hadn't been too keen on the alternative. It wasn't going to be easy to hide with her alone in the wilderness, because while they might have talked things through last night, all the logic and self-preservation in the world didn't change the fact that he still flat-out wanted her.

It was more than physical desire, too—he could have coped with that, he thought, though admittedly he'd never before dealt with this kind of a gut-deep and immediate chemistry. No, there was another level of connection between them, a growing respect and friendship, a camaraderie that tempted him equally, if not more. He wanted to be around her. It was as simple as that, yet not simple at all because they didn't share the same values, didn't want or need the same things.

Their decision the night before had been the right one. But that didn't stop him from being acutely aware of her following close behind him, her movements almost hunter-silent, save for an occasional catch of breath or roll of a pebble or two. And it didn't stop him from remembering the taste of her kiss, the feeling of having her skin against his, and the way her sexy moans had made his blood burn. Which left him more than halfway aroused with his pulse thudding in his ears, low and insistent, and seeming to come from the air around them, as if—

He froze suddenly, lifting a hand to bring her to a stop behind him as he realized that the low churning noise wasn't coming from inside him at all. It was coming from up ahead, maybe even from the other side of the next ridge.

"What is that noise?" she asked in a nearly soundless whisper.

"A generator, maybe." It was definitely engine noise in an area where engine noise had no place being. More, a couple of mottled brown shapes glided overhead, aiming straight for the noise. He glanced back over his shoulder. "Looks like your hypothesis was right on the money, Dr. Bay."

His respect for her brains increased even higher at how it fit together: the copper, the eagles, the militia…even the guy who had originally looked at buying the Forgotten might dovetail in there. Granted, he'd claimed to be looking for gold rather than copper, but right now, Jack's gut said the P.D. should be taking another, closer look at his supposedly kosher background check. Given the way things were going in Bear Claw these days, though, and the chief's reluctance to commit manpower to the backcountry when things were getting bad in the city itself, he would need more proof than just a plausible scenario and some engine noise.

Tori nudged his shoulder with her cell phone. "Let's get in there and take some pictures." When he hesitated, she shook her head. "Don't even try it. The answer is 'No, I won't wait back here while you go reconnoiter.' This is my case, too."

He glanced at her and tried not to wince as he was struck anew by just how tiny she was, her fingers narrow and delicate where they held the phone. He knew from experience, though, that her grip—and her determination—were formidable. And they were just going to go take pictures after all. So he nodded. "Fine. Stay close, keep your head down and do exactly what I say."

She snapped a salute, but her eyes were deadly serious, as was her tone when she said, "I might be brave, but I don't have a death wish. You're in charge, one hundred percent."

He wasn't sure he entirely trusted that would hold true if she got caught up in the moment, but short of handcuffing her to a tree—and thus trapping her if something *did* go wrong—he didn't have much of a choice if he wanted his evidence. So he nodded. "Then follow me. Step where I step, and keep as quiet as possible. We don't know what kind of security perimeter we're dealing with here, so we'll assume the worst and try like hell to stay out of range. All we want is a little look at what's going on down there, nothing more."

And if he kept telling himself that, maybe he would lose the sense that he taking too big of a risk, potentially sacrificing his protectee for the good of the Death Stare case. But the creeping dread stayed firmly in place as they worked their way up the next ridge, with him testing each step and constantly scanning their surroundings, alert for any hint of surveillance devices. Granted, there was no guarantee that he would see the security devices, but he was hoping that whatever outpost they were coming up on was mobile enough that it used a pretty stripped-down perimeter.

The trees on that part of the ridge grew very close together and were badly infected with the fungus, and the hanging strands dragged eerily over the exposed skin of his arms and neck. The trees provided good cover, though, concealing them as they started down the far side of the ridge, headed for where a lighter section up ahead suggested a clearing.

There, engine noise and a low-grade buzz of activity said they had found what they were looking for.

Tori touched his arm briefly, then gestured to the tree-tops, where a dozen or more barred eagles were touching down briefly and then taking wing again, making him think of gulls surrounding a fishing boat and confirming another piece of her hypothesis.

He looked at her and mouthed a soundless *Ready?*

Her eyes were wide and stark in her pale face, but she nodded and lifted her cell phone. He took it, made sure the autoflash was off, and then held it back out to her. Their fingers brushed, and for a second he felt the warmth of that touch throughout his entire body. It made him want to say something to her even though he didn't have a clue what that might be…and he knew he was probably better off leaving it unsaid.

He indulged himself, though, by closing his fingers over hers, folding them around the camera and giving a gentle squeeze. *For luck,* he mouthed, and then made himself let go.

She was still staring after him with a faintly bemused expression when he turned away and headed for the edge of the clearing. Moments later, she fell in behind him, keeping close and moving silently.

The engine noise grew louder, as did the buzz of movement and activity—it wasn't any one definable sound, but rather a sense that there was a lot going on in the clearing. As they approached, he saw that it was actually a natural bowl. That gave him and Tori the advantage of elevation as the trees thinned and camouflaged shapes slowly became visible, their outlines vague and undefined beneath their protective paint jobs and netting.

"Hot damn," he mouthed, whispering the words more to himself than to her. And as his pulse picked up a notch, he realized that he hadn't thought the eagles were going to lead them to the Shadow Militia, not really. But as he and Tori hunkered down at the edge of the depression, hidden behind a pair of gnarled old-man trees as they checked out the scene with the binoculars he'd brought from the wreck, he saw that she had been right on the money.

Below them was spread a mobile encampment of armored vehicles and fat-tired trailers pulled by huge, six-wheeled crawlers. One of the vehicles had a fifty-caliber mounted behind the cab, and another had a neat stack of guns in the back, piled alongside crates he'd bet money contained ammo and other armaments. Figures moved around the vehicles, most with purpose, a few wandering. All were male, under forty and wearing denim, T-shirts and army surplus, with a mix of races and nothing really to suggest a country or cause.

They were all heavily armed, and they moved with the sort of casual swagger he associated with street gangs and the top dogs on a given cell block.

"Son of a bitch," he muttered under his breath, skin crawling at the confirmation that there was a damned private army of some sort hiding in the Forgotten, seemingly right under the noses of the local and federal groups that had been on the hunt for months with no luck… Until now.

Moreover, one of the enclosed trailers had a second, open trailer sitting beside it. The smaller trailer had several huge barrels strapped to it, each in a different color and bearing bright stickers warning that the contents were flammable, acid, volatile and whatnot. Hoses snaked from the containers to the larger trailer, while three big generators were chugging away on the back of a nearby flatbed, feeding thick power cables. Unless he missed his guess, that was the center of whatever they were doing there. And it was something the authorities would very much like to get their hands on.

Tori must have been thinking the same thing because she paused in her picture-taking to grin fiercely up at him, triumph flashing in her expression.

His mind raced. If the militia stayed put for twenty-four hours or so, he'd have time to bring in a team. If not, they could use the eagles to find the next encampment.

Adrenaline zinged through his veins at the dawning knowledge that he and Tori had cracked the case, not only of the fungal infection, but also the Shadow Militia itself. Now all they had to do was reconnect with Tucker and the others and make their report, and the task force would reconvene and take it from there. First, though, they had to get out of there, and keep their heads down until morning.

He touched Tori's arm and tipped his head back the way they had come, mouthing, *Let's go.* She nodded and stowed her cell, and they backed out of their vantage point and started retracing their steps.

Halfway down the ridge, though, he was brought up short by an ominous twig crack. His instinct fired and his heartbeat kicked up a notch, but he stayed still and gestured for Tori to do the same, hoping to hell it was an animal, a random forest noise, something other than—

Crunch-crunch...crunch-crunch.

Damn it. Footsteps. He inhaled and reached for his weapon as the noises came closer.

Breathing softly through his mouth, he urged Tori back away from the noises and their trail, stepping from boulder to boulder in case whoever it was stumbled on their tracks leading in. When they were several hundred yards off their original path, he guided her to a cluster of rocks and gestured her into a somewhat protected niche. Then he put his back to her and unslung his rifle.

"Hey, Ritchie," a man's voice—basso profundo and faintly twangy—called. "You out here?"

Tori flinched and bumped into him, and he tightened his grip on her arm, ready to get a hand across her mouth if she started to panic. But she quickly shook her head, mouthing, *Sorry.*

He let go of her but stayed very close.

"Ritchie? Come on, man, I said I'd cover you for a little while you sparked up, but this is ridiculous. Get your stoned butt back to camp, will you?"

When there was still no answer, the *crack-crunch* resumed, not drawing closer now, but angling away from their position. Jack didn't dare relax, though, because they had to assume that this Ritchie could be somewhere nearby as well.

"Damn it, Ritchie, where are you?" After a pause, there was the hiss of dead air and then the click and silence of someone pushing a radio over to the transmit position. Moments later came a twangy bass complaint of "Denkins, this is Boomer. I can't find Ritchie anywhere. I bet he's been at the product again. Did you check all the sheds?"

Jack couldn't make out the squawk of return radio traffic, but Boomer cursed under his breath and the crunching footfalls resumed, headed back toward the encampment.

When they had faded to silence, Jack safetied his weapons, tucked his nine and reslung his rifle, and took what felt like his first real breath in too long. Then he turned back to Tori, found her pale but resolute, and got a firm nod that said she was good to go. They struck out with him leading the way, sticking to the rocks and heading downhill.

They hadn't gone more than fifty yards when he found the body.

He stopped dead, causing Tori to put a hand on his shoulder to brace herself. "What— Oh!" Her soft gasp of horror sounded very loud, as did the low, vicious curse that hissed through his lips at the sight of the corpse's bulging, terrified eyes.

"Is that…" She trailed off, fingers digging into his shoulder.

"Yeah," he said, forcing the word from a chest gone fiercely hollow all of a sudden. "That's the Death Stare." And he got it. He got it. Damn, he thought as Boomer's comment about the missing man having sampled the product took on a very grim new meaning. "It looks like we've been working on the drug case all along."

The guy—presumably Ritchie—was wearing jeans and a camo jacket with the matching slouchy hat, and had a .38 on his belt. His face was horribly contorted, his skin the sickly greenish gray of death…and his eyes were open and staring, as if he'd spent his last minutes of life in a state of horrible terror.

Death Stare.

The Shadow Militia wasn't using the strange fungus to refine copper ore or searching for gold. They were making drugs from it…and those drugs were killing the inhabitants of his city.

Jack tried not to see Ray's face, tried not to feel the cold burn of rage when he had other things to worry about right then. But it was coming together now, and he didn't like the pattern it was making. Grimly jettisoning crime scene protocol for necessity, he searched the dead man, aware of Tori's wide-eyed stare following him.

"No ID," he reported, "but we've got this." He held up a short-range radio. "He must have turned it off so nobody would bother him while he was getting high." And he had wound up getting dead instead. It was ridiculous to feel bad about that; no doubt when the body made it down to the city, it'd turn out that Ritchie here had a rap sheet and some outstanding warrants. Boy Scouts didn't usually join up with groups like this one.

Banishing the twinge that had hit him anyway, brought on by the sight of that fixed, horrified stare, Jack clicked on the radio and turned the volume up just loud enough for them to hear a clipped, faintly accented voice saying, "My associate failed to take care of the problem, though, which means we need to vacate this site immediately. Pack everything up and lock it all down, gentlemen. We're moving to the alternate site. Make sure the DB-Auto is locked, loaded and ready to go because we're going to have to start over in the new place."

Tori caught his arm so hard that her fingers dug in. "They're going to infect another forest! We have to stop them!"

"No," he said flatly, even though every fiber of his being was screaming *Yes!* He covered her hand with his and pressed down, trapping her touch and bringing her eyes up to his in surprise. He wanted, needed her to look at him and see that he was deadly serious when he said, "We can't risk it, Tori. If they find us, we're dead. And sneaking down there to sabotage their vehicles, send out a distress call using their comm devices or whatever else you're thinking of doing? That would guarantee they would find us." He squeezed her hand. "The world is a better place with you in it. Okay?"

His insides were screaming *Not okay!* but he stuck to his decision. It would cost him, no doubt—in guilt, lost sleep and the faces of the next few to die of the Death Stare—but he refused to endanger Tori in the process of bringing down the Shadow Militia, and he didn't see any other way to do it without revealing their presence.

"What if we could cripple the operation without their realizing we were there?" she asked, uncannily paralleling his thoughts.

"How are you going to manage that?"

She hesitated, blew out a shaky breath and said, "That DB-Auto he mentioned? That's the DNA synthesizer— among other things—they're using to create the fungus. It must need to be built from scratch each time it's released into the wild, and then it can procreate from there. Anyway, the point is that I know how to program DBs... and, better yet, I know how to lock them down."

Chapter Eleven

The sneak attack had been Tori's idea, and she had been the one to convince a reluctant Jack that not only was it worth it—a necessity, in fact—but that it would work. But as she hunkered down behind a couple of fuel canisters in a relatively deserted part of the camp and watched him stroll through the center of the bowl, which was now abuzz with activity where it had been dead before, she was seriously questioning both their judgment and their sanity.

He was nuts to be walking through the Shadow Militia, disguised with little more than the dead man's jacket, a swagger and a surly look. According to him, the encampment was big enough and chaotic enough that he'd pass as one of them long enough to get to the lab trailer and make sure it was secure, so all she would have to do would be to make it from the fuel barrels to the lab, wearing the dead guy's hat and army shirt and keeping her head down.

Piece of cake, right?

Wrong. God, what had she been thinking? She wasn't some sort of superspy; she wasn't even a rookie cop. She was a plant doctor, for heaven's sake! People like her didn't wear disguises cobbled together from a mix of her own outfit and that of a dead man, and they didn't try to cripple high-tech drug rings whose members would stop at nothing to protect their income stream.

"Oh God, oh God, ohGod, ohGodohGodohGod..." The whispered litany was a plea for help, for strength, for luck. Heck, for whatever she could get right now, as Jack stuck his head into the lab trailer, said a few words and then went the rest of the way into the long, narrow room.

She knew he was in there, knew she wasn't alone in the encampment, but with him out of sight she felt suddenly conspicuous, as if a huge floodlight was going to snap on and pin her any second now. Her heart hammered in her chest and sweat bloomed between her breasts and down her spine as she waited for him to come out and give her the all-clear signal.

But what if he didn't come out? What if whoever was in there knew he wasn't one of them? Right now they could be tackling him, restraining him or worse—and her stomach congealed to a cold, hard knot at the thought—what if they killed him outright? Unbidden, her mind superimposed his face on the corpse up on the ridge. Her breath thinned to a pained whistle and her head started to spin.

Don't freak, she told herself. *Slow down. Breathe. You're losing it.*

Even as she tried to breathe slower and hold it together, her brain kept spinning worst-case scenarios. What if their pictures had been circulated around the encampment? What if—

The door to the lab trailer swung open and she jolted so hard that she wound up banging back against one of the fuel containers, which made a hollow, booming noise that sounded incredibly loud to her just then, although it didn't attract any attention from the two rifle-toting men who were nearest her, locked in a low-voiced argument as they strode toward a Humvee that was mounted with the turret gun.

Just as her stress-crazed imagination started showing her images of them firing a barrage into the fuel stockpile where she was hiding, a couple of white-coated men came out of the trailer and headed off to some other destination, and a familiar face with ruggedly handsome features and lake-blue eyes became visible in the shadows of the lab trailer. He sought her out with his gaze, then waved to give her the all clear.

"Jack," she whispered, exhaling a huge gust of relief. "Thank God." She hadn't doubted him, she told herself. Not really. It was more that she had doubted her own luck. Usually with her, when things had a fifty-fifty chance of working out, they went the other way.

Smothering a groan because her knees had locked up while she had crouched there for so long, she rose and emerged from behind the fuel containers, pretending to check the empty clipboard she had grabbed off the fender of one of the Humvees on the way in. She doubted she pulled off the same swagger Jack had used to get across the compound unchallenged, but she kept her hat low and her head down, and minimized the too-feminine sway of her hips as much as she could.

It wasn't that far to the lab trailer, but it seemed to take forever for her to make it across the dusty open space. Her legs felt wooden, the air burned in her lungs and she kept waiting for a shout, a shot, some sort of reaction from the beehive swarm of armed men who eddied around her. But they were busy with their own tasks, their own thoughts, and saw what they expected to see. No one even looked at her funny, at least not that she saw. And then, thank God, she was at the trailer, climbing the three short steps leading to the cool, air-conditioned interior, and the man who was waiting for her there.

Jack pulled her inside, shut and locked the door, and dragged her into his arms.

She stiffened more in delayed reaction than protest, and he let her go and stepped back. "You're right, bad timing. Let's get you to work."

But as he moved away to take up a watchful stance beside the window nearest the door, she stared after him, her heart drumming not just with fear now, but also from sudden heat. The way he had touched her just now was different, and the look in his eye as he glanced over wasn't the same as it had been before. It made her blood hum beneath her skin, bringing new sensitivity and the thought that something had changed between them, though she didn't know what or why.

Or else you're just projecting, she thought wryly. And who could blame her? She would far rather think about her handsome bodyguard than worry about the men outside or the very real possibility that she wouldn't be able to get into the DB's programming. *Man up,* she told herself. And banishing the heat as best she could, she turned and surveyed the lab trailer.

The narrow space was efficiently organized with synthetic and analytical machines at one end, data-crunching stations at the other. Heaps of printouts, binders, boxed supplies and the other odds and ends of a working lab had accumulated at the workstations, suggesting that the R&D phase was over and the main focus was on production. She'd only had hands-on experience with maybe half of the pieces of equipment that were efficiently crammed together in stacked racks, some of which were on air-ride shock absorbers, others already packed with foam and air-filled plastic bumpers to keep them from being damaged when the trailer went mobile.

A few of the machines were still up and running, though, and thank God one of them was her target: the DB-Auto.

"Okay," she said softly, swallowing to wet her suddenly dry mouth as she approached the big, boxy machine. "You can do this." And she could, she had, only never like this before.

The Auto was deceptively plain on the outside, with a user panel that offered little more than a basic keypad, a computer interface and injection ports for various samples and solvents. Inside, though, it contained several robotic arms and a combination of different synthetic and analytical devices that allowed it to offer everything from DNA extraction and analysis to protein synthesis, even in some cases modifying the proteins to near-lifelike end products not normally offered by compact machines.

It was cutting-edge, very expensive...and it had at least one weakness she knew of.

Stretching her fingers like a pianist prepping for the opening chords of a big performance, Tori took a breath, cued up the linked computer terminal and said a quick prayer under her breath as she asked for the main screen of the software, which the company had called DB-Auto-Bahn, even though its speed was more in the category of "middle lane stuck behind a heavily loaded truck." When the screen popped up, all blue and white and vaguely cartoonish, just like she'd expected, she exhaled. "Thank you, Mr. Scientist, whoever you are."

"Good news?" Jack said from his surveillance post.

"It's not pass-coded, which is going to save time." She dropped down into the guts of the software and got to work, clicking and typing, changing a line here, a number there. All the while, she was aware of him dividing his attention between the window and her progress.

"I'm impressed. Maybe you should add 'hacker' to your résumé."

"Nope, I can only really mess with this one machine." She kept going as she spoke, aware that the seconds were ticking by far too quickly. "One of my old bosses actually was a pretty good hacker. Unfortunately, he also had a really mean sense of humor, and he liked to test the people around him, to see if they were worthy of his supposed greatness. Now and then, he would go in and reprogram some of the machines to give bogus answers, produce slightly altered products, that sort of thing. Then he'd get angry if we didn't catch it."

"Sounds like a real prize to work for."

She made a face as she guessed wrong, hit a dead end and had to backtrack. "He was a brilliant scientist and I learned a ton from him. But, yeah, he wasn't my favorite human being ever." She paused as things started flowing again. "Guess I owe him for this one, though, because rather than getting paranoid about our science, the way he wanted us to, we figured out how to undo his little programming tweaks and came up with ways to shut him out of the programs entirely so he couldn't mess with them anymore. Which is what—" she hit the final two keys "—I've done here."

His eyebrows lifted. "That was fast."

"I'm not in the mood to stick around." Returning the Auto to its sleep settings, she pushed away from the console, the memories of past labs—safe jobs—draining as their surroundings came back into focus around her, bringing a renewed sense of urgency. "Let's get out of here."

"Your wish is my... Damn it." His voice and features hardened. "Someone's coming this way." He reached out a hand for her as she crossed the room. When she took it, he drew her close and said into her ear in an undertone, "Play along, and whatever you do, don't look at anyone. Keep your head down, you hear me?"

When she nodded, heart pounding sickly in her ears and sudden terror welling up from wherever it had briefly subsided to, he dragged down her hat so it practically covered her eyebrows and, without warning, dropped her hand and yanked open the door.

"Lazy good for nothing," he snarled, grabbing her collar and shoving her out, so she stumbled down the steps and practically plowed into the two guys who were just about to start up them.

The men—not the lab-coated figures that Jack had talked into leaving the lab trailer earlier, but rather two more toughs of the armed-and-dangerous variety—scowled and fell back. "What the hell?" one demanded, reaching for her arm.

Jack yanked her away on the pretext of shaking her, giving a growl of, "Can't believe you made me look like an idiot back there. And what the hell were you thinking, sneaking into the big trailer like that?" To the men, he said as an aside, "Sorry, won't happen again."

"Wait," one said, going for his radio.

"Can't," Jack fired back. "This moron's already made me late as spit."

Her breath wheezed in her lungs and she fought to keep her footing as he hustled her along, heading for the fuel stash she'd been hiding in before. They drew some attention, but nobody tried to stop them, and the two guys in the lab trailer didn't raise an alarm. In fact, there wasn't the slightest ripple of a response as they reached the fuel, bypassed the big drums and headed up the incline of the bowl, aiming for the tree line.

Either the members of the Shadow Militia were so focused on their own tasks as the camp got ready to evac, or they were used to seeing senior soldiers dragging hapless underlings into the forest for punishment. Tori didn't know why, but the suspicion that the latter was particularly true really reached inside and grabbed on, as did the utter strangeness of having fiddled with a DB-Auto—a normal, everyday machine—under such completely nonordinary circumstances.

She had walked into and out of an armed encampment. She had fried their Auto, or at least locked it down tight enough that it would not only refuse to work now, but it would also refuse to release any of the info stored in its databanks. She had bumped into a guy wearing a machine gun slung over his shoulder.

The ground pitched suddenly beneath her and the sky began to spin. She grabbed on to Jack, who still had her by the arm, and was hustling them up the slope of the next ridge. "Oh, God," she wheezed, "I think I'm going to…"

"Not yet." He changed his grip, looping her hand over his neck and wrapping an arm around her waist, supporting her so that her feet were barely touching the ground.

"Stay with me, sweetheart. We need to get far enough away that we'll have a head start if they sound the alarm."

She let herself lean on him. "Sorry. I'm sorry. I don't mean to be a wimp."

He shot her a look she was too strung-out to interpret. "Don't be sorry. And you're not a wimp. You're about the furthest from a wimp I can imagine."

"For a civilian," she said thinly.

"For anyone." He nudged her to a cluster of dull gray rocks within the shield of a thick stand of fungus-infected trees. "Okay, we're going to stop here for a little while. Now you can feel free to faint, puke, have quiet hysterics…whatever you need to do. I won't judge, I promise."

She sank down gratefully with her back against one of the big boulders, and rested her forehead on her knees while she concentrated on breathing. *In. Out. In. Out.*

Beyond the small-feeling cage created by her body, she was conscious of Jack taking a quick prowl around the immediate area. Once he was reassured that they were as safe as they were likely to get right then, he sat down and leaned back against a rock opposite her, then stretched out his long legs on one side of her, close enough that she could feel the warmth of his body heat. Or maybe she just thought she could. Either way, it helped. It mattered. He was something solid and real when nothing else seemed that way right then.

In. Out. In. Out.

He pulled out the stolen radio and clicked it on, dialing through the channels to check whether there were other conversations going on. Finding just the one airwave in use, he settled on it, tuned the squelch and settled back to listen in on the chatter, which was focused on securing the last of the trailers to move out; checking maps but not revealing the coordinates of the "alternate site"; and berating somebody named Bert for being an idiot and denting one of the trailers with a Humvee.

"Sounds like we're in the clear," Jack said to her.

His voice was clear and undistorted, as if he was looking right at her. She didn't want to think about the picture she probably made—huddled, bedgraggled, wearing a dead man's hat and shirt—didn't want to think about anything really, so she nodded without looking up, and concentrated on breathing. Nice and steady. Breathing meant she was alive. Slow and steady meant she was okay.

In. Out. In. Out. In. Out.

After a minute or two more of that, the spins slowed and then receded, and she lost the need to faint, puke or have quiet hysterics. Instead, chilled, she crossed her arms, curled into herself, and concentrated on not rocking back and forth like the traumatized survivor of some mass tragedy when really, they had been damn lucky so far.

Hopefully that luck would hold. Either way, though, she needed to pull herself together. Just because she could trust Jack to look out for her didn't mean she should give him too much work to do in that regard.

Exhaling a long, shuddering breath, she uncoiled, straightening to lean back against her rock and look at him. He was still wearing the camouflage jacket over his ragged button-down and jeans. The faux-military look probably should have given her the shakes after what they had just been through—and the fact that he was wearing dead guy clothes—but instead, her system leveled off at the sight of him, the reality of him.

When their eyes met, a frisson of awareness moved

through her, reminding her of the impression she'd gotten back in the lab, that something was different. His gaze had always been direct and confident, but now it seemed more wholly focused on her.

"You okay?" he asked.

Perhaps for the first time with him, she didn't weigh her answer for wimpiness before giving it. "I'm shaky."

He tipped his head. "Me, too."

"I doubt that, but appreciate the thought." She paused, swallowing to clear the gritty taste of stale fear. "Do you think it's safe to go back to the crash site?"

Glancing at the radio, he considered the question for a moment, then tipped his hand in a "maybe" gesture that leaned toward the affirmative side. "The way I figure it, worst-case scenario is that the first transmission we over-heard, the one about a business associate not getting the job done, means they went looking to confirm that we died in the crash, and know that we didn't. But given that their response to that was to order an evac, and they don't know yet that we messed with their equipment, they don't have any new reason to come after us. Not to mention that they probably assumed we tried to hike out, or maybe got picked up already."

"They could have tracked us from the crash," she said, not yet ready to feel reassured.

"If they did that, they would have known we headed for the encampment." He shook his head. "No, I really think we're going to be okay here, Tori. We'll keep the radio on and our eyes open, obviously, and we'll set a hell of a perimeter around wherever we camp, and make damn sure there are a couple of ways out...but unless some-thing changes drastically, I think our best bet is going to be going back toward the site, grabbing our gear from the cache and finding someplace to hole up for the night."

She thought about it for a moment, but couldn't see a better option, and couldn't really fault his logic. "Okay, I'm in. But first…" Reaching over, she tugged on the sleeve of the camo jacket. "Should we get this stuff back to the dead guy, in case they look a little harder for him, and actually find him this time?"

"Good thinking." He paused, glancing in the direction of the corpse. "You want to hunker down here and I'll go take care of it?"

She suppressed a shudder at the thought of the man's bug-eyed stare and silent scream, but shook her head. "Thanks, but I'm coming with you, partner."

That earned her a raised eyebrow, but he didn't comment or contradict. Instead, he nodded slowly. "Okay, then, partner. Let's get moving."

THEY RETURNED the dead man's clothes and set off for the crash site with Jack in the lead. He kept them roughly parallel to their original track and watched intently for signs that they were being followed, but didn't see any red flags. More, just before they got all the way out of radio range of the encampment, the chatter indicated that the Shadow Militia was moving out.

Part of him hated like hell to hear that because the bastards had disappeared into thin air before, which meant there was a chance they were about to do it again. Granted, he and Tori had a ton of new info to add to the conversation, but still, there were no guarantees.

That was the thing, though, wasn't it? Life didn't come with guarantees.

Maybe that wasn't the most original revelation ever, but hell, he'd never claimed to be all that original a guy. He had followed the family tradition by playing high school football, joining the Bear Claw P.D. and then marrying his high school sweetheart—or at least trying to. And when that last part hadn't worked out the way he'd hoped it would, he'd tried to find a woman the same way he built most of his cases, piece by piece and detail by detail, trying to make it all fit every step along the way. But just as there was no guarantee that methodical policework would solve every case, there was no saying that the slow-and-steady approach would bear fruit either. It sure hadn't done so yet.

When he came down to it, he'd solved a handful of his most successful and most satisfying cases through luck and lightning-strike flashes of intuition rather than doggedness. Which meant…hell, he didn't know what it meant in relation to Tori, but he knew one thing for damn sure: watching her shuffle across the encampment, out there in the open by herself, where any number of guys within a hundred feet of her could have caught on and gunned her down before he drew a bead, had been one of the worst things he'd ever lived through. And the knowledge that she could have died dozens of times over out there had slapped him across the face with his not-so-original revelation, along with the addendum that given the lack of guarantees in life, he should be careful not to miss out on something special because he was too set in old patterns that didn't always work.

Tori might be a flash of lightning rather than an eyewitness statement, but through the course of a solid and satisfying career, it was the lightning flashes that stood out and made him smile. Why hadn't he seen that before?

"We're getting close to the cache, aren't we?" she asked from behind him, sounding slightly winded but far stronger than she had right after their escape from the encampment.

Sure enough, when he looked back at her, her eyes had traded dull shock for focus, and her lips had gone from being pinched and on the verge of trembling to a bow of determination. Warmth and respect centered in his chest in a devastating one-two punch, and he thought again of lightning.

"Yeah, it's just over that next ridge and off to the west." Forcing himself to focus on their surroundings—because if a trap had been set, this would be the place—he got his rifle off his back and used the sight to scan the area. When nothing set off warning bells, he continued onward with her right behind him, both of them treading carefully and staying alert.

They reached the cache without incident, retrieved their gear and then moved higher up the cliff above the roadway to a cave he'd scouted earlier. With a wide mouth, a crevice leading out the back, an eagle's-eye view of the roadway and the busted-up SUV and a flat, wind-smoothed floor, it fit the bill of an overnight campsite, and then some.

Together, they set a security perimeter, then pulled out the basics for an overnight, setting up an efficient, workable camp with minimal hassle, moving around each other as if they'd done this a hundred times before. And although she'd been the one to say the word, it really did feel like a partnership.

How long had it been since he'd had a partner? The

rookies didn't count, and even his two prior detective-grade partners had been more along the lines of guys he hooked up with for this case or that, while working on his own most of the time. As for women...yeah, he'd dated, even had relationships. But a partner? He hated to admit it, but he had to go back to college and the first few years after, when he and Kayla had done the same things, wanted the same things.

It hadn't escaped him that Tori had a lot of the qualities he'd loved the most about Kayla back then: she was smart, sassy, spunky and not afraid of dirt, sweat or bugs. Better yet, Tori had brought those qualities into her adult life rather than outgrowing them, and she didn't apologize for that, or anything else really.

She had a bone-deep integrity he admired and a grit that had seen her through the day they'd just had. If she could get through that and still be focused now, she should be able to do most anything. Which made him picture her back out in the Forgotten with him, only this time there wasn't any militia and the trees weren't sick; it was just the two of them, their backpacks and the mountains for as long as they wanted to stay out there together.

And he so shouldn't be thinking along those lines. Especially not when he was supposed to be assembling the collapsible propane stove they were going to use in lieu of starting a too-bright, too-smoky fire.

Not wanting to know how long he'd been sitting there, staring off into space, he bent over the disassembled stove and got to work. He was so intent on the job that it took him a minute to realize that Tori was sitting motionless a few feet away from him with a couple of carbon dioxide ampoules and the second of the inflatable mattresses in front of her. And she was staring at him—not accusingly, but rather bemusedly, as if she were coming to some startling new revelation.

Yeah. He knew how that felt.

"Listen," he began. "I've been thinking—" He didn't get any further, though, because she gave a small, strangled sob, lurched across the short distance separating them, and kissed him.

It wasn't a kiss of passion so much as one of connection, affirmation. Her lips were closed, her hands fisted in his shirt and hair, her body sprawled partly atop his.

Surprise was quickly followed by the heat that hadn't fully died since the night before when he'd truly gotten a taste of her. More, there was exultation because this wasn't the cautious, reserved Tori who had ridden up the mountain with him, not making eye contact. Now she clung to him, shaking, as if things had changed for her, too.

She broke the kiss and pressed her forehead to his as she whispered, "I'm so glad it was you there with me today. If it hadn't been…" Drawing in a shuddering breath, she shook her head slightly, the movement transmitting from her to him through the slide of skin against skin. She pulled away and kissed his cheek. "Thank you."

"Enough." Even as his blood burned from the caresses, he eased away from her, catching her wrists so she couldn't go too far as she drew back, surprised, her cheeks going from the pink of desire to the deeper flush of mounting embarrassment. "No," he said when she started to say something, "it's my turn. I don't want to argue semantics with you, so I'll start by saying 'You're welcome' and that yeah, I did my job. But you've got to know that you stopped being a job that first night, Tori, when you held it together during the shooting and then refused to leave when your bosses pulled the plug. And every day since then, guarding you has been less about the job and more about me admiring your determination and wanting to help your investigation in any way possible." He paused as she went even wider-eyed, then went ahead and said, "Plus, it's been about protecting you because I don't want to imagine a world without your energy and enthusiasm in it… And most of all, I've been right there with you every step of the way these past few days because there's nowhere else I'd rather be." He paused. "I want to be here for you, Tori. I want to be with you."

Her eyes darkened. "But last night…"

"Was last night, and I think the things that have happened today have put what's going on between the two of us in a different light. At least they have for me." He raised an eyebrow in question.

She nodded slowly, new color flooding her face, coming not from embarrassment this time, he thought, but from desire. "Me, too." It was a whisper but carried the force of a shout.

Heat leaped within him, flaring from the lust he'd been suppressing for days, which already eclipsed the feelings he'd had for any of the women he'd dated in the past few years. This was it, he thought. She was what he'd been waiting for, what he'd needed. Who would have guessed it?

Not him, that was for sure. But while they might not look like they should work given the evidence, the lightning said he needed to make the leap. So he shifted, touched his lips to hers and took them both under with a kiss that had nothing to do with gratitude or the adrenaline of having gotten into and out of the encampment undetected, and everything to do with the two of them, then and there.

When he pulled away, her eyelid fluttered open to reveal pupils dilated with desire. Still, though, need, tension and a hint of nerves strung him tight as he said, "Will you lie down with me, sweet Tori, and finish what we started last night?"

Chapter Twelve

Tori. Couldn't. Breathe.

It was a first for her really. Always before, she'd rolled with the flow of an encounter, letting it stay simple and casy. But there was nothing simple about the way her heart shuddered in her chest, and there was nothing easy about the emotions that churned inside her. Because she might have thought last night that she could be Jack's lover for as long as it felt right, and then walk away unscathed, but in the light of day she knew differently.

She liked and respected him, had gotten attached to him, and it was the attachment that worried her. Kneeling there on the sandy cave floor, in a universe that suddenly seemed to have contracted down to the two of them and the question that hung between them, she couldn't remember what it had felt like to be anywhere else, couldn't remember wanting to be with anyone else.

Who are you and what have you done with the real Tori Bay?

She didn't have an answer for that. Worse, she wasn't sure she cared just then, wrapped in Jack's arms with her lips moist from his kisses and her ears ringing with the rasping request that suddenly seemed like the sexiest, most romantic thing a man had ever said to her.

He was meeting her on her terms, wanting to be with her tonight, in the indefinite "now" that had them here together, and safe, thanks to him.

He might not want her gratitude, but he had it. Without him, she wouldn't have been able to stay on the case, wouldn't have seen the glory of Bear Claw Canyon at sunrise, wouldn't have put all the pieces of the investigation together into the workable, if terrifying, hypothesis that they needed to bring back down to the city. And she most certainly wouldn't have lived long enough for the hypothesis to matter.

The heat pumping in her veins now didn't come from gratitude, though, or from her bone-deep relief at being alive. Both of those things were inside her, of course… but the flames of desire were so much stronger, overriding even the part of her that wanted to recall that they'd had good reasons for sleeping in separate beds last night.

She wanted what he was offering: her. Him. The two of them together in the small, safe place he had made for them.

"Yes." The word was a breath, a shape of lips that barely grazed each other.

His eyes fired and his fingers tightened where they were splayed at her hip and shoulder, but he held back. She could feel the effort it cost him in the rigid tension of his arms and neck, hear it in the rasp of his voice as he said, "Tell me."

Her stomach coiled on a surge of desire that left her wet and aching. She took a breath that did nothing to settle the inner churn, and said, "I want this, Jack. I want to make love with you."

Triumph and fierce, flattering joy lashed across his features, and then his lips came down on hers in a kiss that was equally ferocious and joyful, and made her heart sing. Her pulse stuttered as their tongues touched and slid, and his hands found their way to her waistband and then beneath her shirt. His fingertips were hot on her skin, and the faint rasp of masculine calluses sent new heat flaring from the points of contact and outward, curling to her breasts and bringing a blush of moisture to her cleft with a poignant intensity that had her sagging against him with a soft moan.

He growled a low curse, earthy and reverent, and caught her up against his chest, gathering her close and lifting her easily as he rose to his feet. Under any other circumstance, with any other man, she would have raised hue and cry at the idea of being carried anywhere. Now, though, his powerful move reminded her of the way he'd swaggered across the encampment, walking among their enemies without flinching. The memory—and the echo of fear it brought—had her tightening her arms around his neck and pressing her cheek to his.

He lowered her gently to the air mattress she had already inflated and padded further with one of the two sleeping bags that had been among the supplies they'd been carrying around in the SUV. More than once, she had inwardly rolled her eyes at the mountain of gear that Jack and his ranger friend had deemed necessary for their daily trips into the Forgotten.

Now, though, she was grateful for the forethought… and the softness at her back as he followed her down and eased alongside her, so they were facing each other, bodies aligned.

Last night he had wanted to dissect things, as if trying

to talk himself into—or out of—a decision. Now, though, with the decision made, he said nothing as he cupped her cheek, leaned in and took her mouth with a kiss that was somehow sweet, gentle and possessive all at the same time.

If their prior kisses had been storms—all thunder and passion—this one was a love song that made her want to believe in forever, at least for a little while. She shuddered and clutched at him even as she did her best to return the seduction and give as good as she was getting. Which was very good indeed.

Maybe a small but persistent alarm was going off inside her, warning that she was in too deep, that she needed to pull back and regain her normal perspective. If so, she ignored it because she trusted Jack and he knew the score. They would be fine.

"So sweet," he murmured, then kissed her lips, her cheeks, then blazed a path down her throat to the hollow of her neck to nuzzle there, planting soft, insistent kisses that tightened her skin and set off starbursts behind her closed eyelids.

She tipped her head back, exposing herself to his lips, and luxuriated in the sensations as his hands skimmed up beneath her shirt and found her breasts and the hard points of her nipples, which he worked in rhythm with his kisses and the gentle roll of his body against hers. Her shirt came off and then his, and they were belly to belly, skin to skin, and although she was caressing him, kissing him, learning his body and the places where her touch could make him shiver and groan, he was utterly in charge, dominating her, not with his superior size or strength, but with the things he was making her feel.

Warning. Dangerous.

This time she heard the alarm, heeded it, knowing that she didn't dare give any man power over her, even one she trusted as much as she trusted this one. And this wasn't the hot and heavy lovemaking she had expected based on the explosive kisses they had shared leading up to this point. He was worshipping her, imprinting himself on her. She felt entirely feminine, entirely wanted. But she also felt naked and needy, and knew that if he got up and walked away at that moment, she would have watched him leave. Worse, she might even have asked him to stay.

The realization put her off-kilter. Or maybe she'd been that way since the night before, unable to regain her balance when things hadn't gone the way she had hoped they would.

They were going that way now, though. Which meant it was time to put the two of them back on more even footing.

"Hey," she said, bringing his eyes up from the V of her breasts, "my turn."

Before he could anticipate the move, she shifted up and over him, bearing him back beneath her. He had proven aptly before that he could handle her weight, but he let her have the leverage, lying back and looking up at her with a heated expression that she interpreted as *Bring it on.*

Excitement flared in her bloodstream and the warning smoothed to a cautionary note as she rose above him and kissed his jaw, his throat and then shifted lower, trailing her lips along the downward-pointing arrow of masculine hair on his leanly muscled chest and washboard abs.

He arched and groaned—a short, sharp noise that reverberated off their rocky surroundings—and his hands came up to cradle her head. His fingers sifted through her hair, flexing as her lips cruised along the verge of his waistband and she lightly scraped her fingernails down his thighs.

She might have intended to seduce him and equal the balance of pleasure between them, but as she trailed her hands back up, stroking the strong columns of muscle and absorbing his groan, she was thoroughly seduced herself.

Her blood burned as she palmed the long line of his erection, which strained tautly beneath his jeans and then, when she loosened them and tugged down his boxers, sprang free into her hands. Her breath trembled when she took in the long length of him, ruddy and engorged for her, with a thick, corded vein that throbbed in time with the fast, excited beat of his heart. And her inner muscles pulsed, yearned, when she encircled him with her hand, covering the wide, blunt tip of his hardness and then taking a long stroke downward, reveling in his harsh groan and the way he shifted restlessly against her, thoroughly at her mercy as she touched him, worked him, stroked him and brought him breathlessly to the edge, and wound up bringing herself there as well.

Passion flowed through her, tightening her core yet relaxing her mind, until she didn't care that her head was spinning and she wasn't entirely herself anymore. She only cared about the rushing heat inside her, the presage to an orgasm brought solely by his restless hands and the fierce joy of making him feel the same sort of heat that pounded inside her with an increasing tempo that would soon demand release.

Then his hands shifted to her shoulders and he urged her back up his body. "Come here," he murmured. "Let me."

Before she could return through the sensuous haze to

regain full control of herself, he was kissing her, caressing her, loosening his clothes and hers, and then tugging them free until they were both naked beneath the blanket, which let in wisps of the chilling mountain air as they moved, twining together while he caressed her exquisitely sensitive breasts and then down to her hips, her thighs and finally to the wet, wanting place between.

She arched against him and gasped into his mouth when his fingers found her, parted her moist folds, and slipped between, setting up a delicious friction that brought her trembling once more to the brink. Refusing to go there alone, she stroked his hard flesh. Her touch wrung a sharp hiss out of him, had him surging into her hand with a harsh whisper of, "Ah, Tori."

Unaccountable pressure tightened around her heart, and her eyes misted at the sudden sure knowledge that he knew exactly who she was in that moment, that she wasn't just a pleasurable interlude as she had been for too many of her prior lovers. Knowing, too, that it had been the same way for her too often before—nice guys, no harm, no foul, no investment—she pressed her cheek to his and whispered, "Jack."

She would have said something more, would have told him how good he was making her feel or what she wanted to do to him next, but the words backed up in her throat, locked there by the intensity of his next kiss and the spiraling pleasure being aroused by his fingers. She bowed into his touch with a wordless cry as he quickened the rhythm of his touch and she did the same, until they were gasping and twining together, grinding toward the pinnacle.

He shifted over her, rose above her, and then, going a bit wild-eyed, looked around them. "Where's the—"

"Here." She popped the top off the first aid kit and offered the small box of condoms she'd noticed there earlier.

Grinning, he donned the protection with an aside of "Remind me to thank Blackthorn for the supplies."

"I'll thank him myself," she retorted, not letting herself feel a pang that she would probably never meet the ranger in person. This wasn't about what might or might not happen tomorrow, after all. It was about the two of them, here and now.

Finished with the necessary task, he lowered himself until his body just brushed hers with feather-light touches that teased and incited almost as much as the kisses he dusted onto her throat, her face and then finally her lips.

Not to be outdone—or have them put off balance once more—she curled her legs around his, and arched upward to slide herself along his length, finding him hard and ready, and the normally cool slickness of latex gone warm and taut against his body, fading to insignificance in the face of the pleasure that spiraled through her when he groaned into her mouth and surged against her in a primal, instinctive response to her caress.

She gasped at the flood of sensations, then moaned when he repeated the move, rolling his hips into hers so his hardness dragged back and forth across her cleft and the sensitive folds within.

"Oh!" She let her head fall back, let her body move with his, back and forth, back and forth, until the orgasm that had earlier flirted without delivering now came back to hover just out of reach, waiting for him to fill the aching hollow inside her.

As his next stroke began, she shifted her hips, angling

so that he slid deeper and seated himself in the natural pocket formed by her body.

Groaning, he slowed his thrust and then stopped, so he was poised just at the outer ring of the achingly heated flesh that was so very moist and ready for him. And then, inch by smooth, fulfilling inch, he sheathed himself to the hilt. Then he paused there, pressed his temple to hers as their breathing heaved in synchrony and their bodies vibrated with the intimate joining.

She shuddered at the delicious invasion, mouth opening in a round, soundless O of delight as his entry set off bursts of color behind her closed eyelids, detonations of heat and pleasure within her. Then, moving a little beneath him, she curled her feet around behind his calves and used the leverage to press up against him and take him just that little bit deeper, until he was hitting her sweet spots inside and out, intensifying sensations that were already almost unbearably intense.

A moan slipped from her lips and he caught it with his mouth as he shifted to kiss her wetly, deeply, one kiss leading to another and another, taking her deeper and deeper still as he withdrew and then came back into her on a powerful surge that hit those same spots. She arched and gasped in surprise as he did it again, proving that the move had been no accident.

Always before, she'd had to find that doubled pleasure herself, by making sure that she had the depth and angle right while her partner thrust as suited him. Jack, though, had not only taken the hint, he was running with it, expanding on it, experimenting with slightly different angles and depths, and gauging her responses.

His athlete's body surged against hers, sure and strong.

She moaned at the building sensations and her hands splayed open on his back as pleasure robbed her of the ability to do much more than hold on and counterpoint his thrusts with an instinctive rhythm of her own that made him growl her name low at the back of his throat.

They rocked together, and the heat built within her. They kissed, and needs coiled tighter and tighter still. When he rasped her name and pressed his forehead to hers, she felt powerful, and when his thrust worked that secret inner spot that drove her wild, she could moan and cling, because she felt safe with him.

Passion swept over her like a spring storm at high altitude, powerful and lovely, leaving her breathless with the climb. She dug her fingers into the strong columns of muscle on either side of his spine, helpless to do anything other than ride the surging ascent as she rocketed up, up, up...and then hung poised.

In that moment, she was wholly aware of her own body and his, and the way they fit together. Then the quiet shattered into a tingling chorus of pleasure that contracted inward around his hard, driving flesh as he rasped her name once more, and then exploded outward, toppling her from the high altitude she had attained and plunging her into the vibrating waves of a huge orgasm.

The starbursts of color behind her eyelids went to red and then blurred to gray as every fiber of her being concentrated itself at the point of their joining. Her inner muscles closed around him, worked him, milked him, and she whispered, "Oh, *Jack*."

He stiffened and bucked against her, once, twice and a third time, and then he let out an inarticulate noise and sank into her, against her, grinding with delicious thrusts as he came, shuddering and groaning her name. His pleasure prolonged hers, sending the delicious tension spiraling through her once more. She wrapped her arms around his waist, pressed her face into the side of his neck and reveled in the sensations as her orgasm faded to aftershocks, and then to a deep, drugging, warm afterglow of satisfaction.

They lay like that, wrapped together and breathing in synchrony, for a long time. Long enough that their bodies cooled and she started to notice the chill mountain air.

She must have shivered, or else she and Jack were on the same wavelength, because he lifted off her, shifted them so they were on their sides facing each other, dealt with the condom and then brought up the blanket and tucked them in together with a gentle thoroughness that made her heart give a little *thudda-thudda*.

It was tempting to burrow into him, close her eyes and doze. She didn't want to analyze a sexual encounter that had catapulted right into her top-five list—she wasn't willing to really think any further than that—but it was inevitable, wasn't it? So as her brain started to come back online, bringing with it new nerves and a sense that what they had just done together might not have been her best move ever, she stirred against him, starting to rouse.

"Don't," he said softly. "Not yet."

Her eyes flew open. "What?"

"Don't think about it. Just let it be for tonight. Okay?"

Body easing of a tension she hadn't even consciously recognized until that moment, she smiled softly. "I thought that was my line."

"Maybe I've learned a couple of things in the past few days." He kissed the corners of her mouth, expression serious but not dire, and more relaxed than she'd seen him before. She was struck anew by the mountain-lake-blue of his gorgeous eyes, and remembered noticing them that first time in the airport and thinking he was way out of her usual league.

Apparently, she'd been promoted, at least temporarily. And thank God for that.

"Okay." She blew out a breath, letting go of more of the unacknowledged tension. "Yeah. Okay." Then, flushing a little at the loss of her usual postcoital no-harm-no-foul cool, she said, "That was pretty special."

"That's because you're pretty special."

She wasn't sure which was worse, the fact that he said it with a bit too much feeling, stirring low-grade nerves in her belly…or the fact that hearing it made her want to cuddle into him and bask in the shared warmth of their bodies, the shared afterglow of their lovemaking. Which wasn't her usual style, not by a long shot.

It wasn't a hard-and-fast rule that she didn't spend the night with her lovers, or vice versa, but it was a rare event. Here, though, although she could blame it on the cave and the danger, the reality was that she would have wanted to stay regardless. Which was usually her cue to leave.

"You're doing it again."

She snapped her gaze back to his. "Doing what?"

"Thinking. I've got a better idea for what we can do instead."

Arching an eyebrow, even though it didn't take a rocket scientist—or a plant doctor—to guess what he had in mind, she said, "Oh, really? Why don't you whisper it in my ear?"

She was aiming for playful, but that got derailed when

he leaned in, cupped one of her breasts in his wide, warm palm and told her, in explicit detail, exactly what he wanted to do. As he spoke, her breath came short, her nipples peaked and she shuddered with a new wash of longing made even more intense than before because she knew now what it felt like to be with him.

This time she heard the warning bells loud and clear: they said she needed to ease back and regain control of both herself and their encounter.

Before that thought could fully form, though, he rose over her, pressed his body full-length against hers, and took her mouth in a long, slow, drugging kiss that sent her floating once more, awash in a storm of sensation and desire. On some level she told herself that this was a bad idea, that she shouldn't let it go on like this. But as his hands moved up her body, caressing and inciting with achingly slow gentleness, she melted, unable to remember why the balance between them even mattered.

So she softened against him, letting him be in charge, and felt an added frisson of excitement at the realization that she could do that with him. She trusted him that much.

As if realizing what she was giving up to him, what it meant, he caught her face in his hands, murmured her name and pressed his lips to hers in a chaste kiss that somehow said *Thank you,* or maybe *I won't let you down.* And if the second sentiment brought a quiver of nerves, they were quickly swept away by heat and longing when he kissed her again and, without warning or preamble, positioned himself to slide into her once more.

She felt the slick heat of a fresh rubber, the hard pulse of fresh need, and parted her legs for him, inviting him inside. He seated himself on a powerful thrust that tugged at her out-of-practice muscles even as it brought new pleasure spiraling inside her. She would have moved with him, urged him on, even set the pace, but when she shifted to get a hand between their bodies, he caught her wrists, drew her arms around his neck, and said softly, "Let me love you."

Again, a quiver of nerves. Again, lost in the heat of desire.

He kissed her over and over, and all the while moved within her, with thrusts that began as slow hip-roll pulses and built from there. As before, he absorbed her responses and used the information to bring her pleasure spiraling higher and higher still. Now, though, it seemed he was anticipating those responses because he touched her in all the right places, stroked her with exactly the perfect pressure and speed. And where with another man all that attention to the details might have seemed calculated, coming from him it made her chest ache with the knowledge that he was paying attention to her, thinking about her. Only her.

He caressed her, kissed her, thrust into her…and he made love to her, well and truly.

She had long called the act by that name, but now the two words took on a new and deeper meaning for her. On one level, she knew that should be a terrifying concept to the woman she'd worked so hard to make herself into. On another, though, she couldn't find any terror amid the passion. She burned beneath his touch, coming alive in a second orgasm that caught her by surprise, sliding through her on a long, rolling wave of pleasure that leveled off but didn't subside. Instead, her senses hung poised as his tempo quickened and his breathing increased, and he started to thrust in a new and determined rhythm.

"Yes," she whispered. "Oh, yes. Yes, yes, yesyesyes!" Another orgasm washed through her, or maybe this one was a continuation of the last; she didn't know. All she knew was that the right answer for her, then and there, was to tighten her arms around his neck, press her cheek to his and ride out the huge, pleasurable waves as he shuddered and came deep inside her, with an orgasm that, like the act itself, seemed somehow far more meaningful than it ever had for her before.

And this time when they lay cooling once more, she didn't have to work at keeping her brain quiet; it just *was* quiet. She was content to lie there in his arms, warm, drowsy and drifting, and listening to the sounds of the night falling around them.

She was, so very atypically, content to just *be*.

Even later, after the lethargy passed and they got up and moved around a little, smiling softly when their eyes met or their bodies brushed in passing, they didn't really talk about what was happening between them. And the same held true when, long after dark and working by the illumination of tiny flashlights that they used as sparingly as possible, they finished assembling the stove and cooked a decent camp dinner by the dim glow of the propane burner. They talked, of course—about the meal, the terrain, a bit about their respective childhoods, but not about them.

That was just fine with her. They had talked enough last night for any two of her other relationships, maybe three, and they had their ground rules, so they didn't need to discuss any of it further. And she didn't want to talk about the case or about what was going to happen tomorrow. If tonight was the only time they were going to have before their higher-ups insisted that she leave Bear Claw for her own safety, then she wanted it to just be about the two of them.

And it was. It was just the two of them as they sand-scoured the dishes and packed them away, and it was just the two of them as they sat outside the cave mouth for a while, wrapped in a blanket and cuddled together to watch the impossibly starry sky. And it was just the two of them as they returned to the air mattress, which should have seemed far too small for them both but somehow didn't.

They dozed, woke, made love and then fell asleep for real or at least Tori did, because the next thing she knew, she was being nudged awake, confused and disoriented to find herself wrapped around a warm, naked male body. She reared back and blinked up into lake-blue eyes that looked far more awake that she was, and were filled with warm affection and, she thought, an undercurrent of wary regret.

Memory returned quickly, and with it came a throb that wasn't quite horror, but wasn't all that far off.

Oh, boy. Oh, boy. Ohboyohboyohboy. She had done it; she had made love with Jack. She had spent the night with him, was waking up with him, had let him in deeper than anyone since…heck, deeper than anyone ever before. Nerves pinged through her and her heartbeat accelerated to a fast *thump-thump-thump* that seemed to echo in the cave, until she realized the noise *was* echoing in the cave, and it wasn't her heart.

Glancing out through the cave mouth, where it was full daylight, the dawn long gone while she'd slept in her temporary lover's arms. She couldn't see what was making the noise, but as her head cleared, her stomach knotted on the sure knowledge of what she was hearing.

It was a helicopter. Morning had come, and with it, their rescue. It was time for them to return to reality.

She looked back at him, met his eyes and saw the knowledge there that they weren't going to get a chance to postmortem what had turned out to be the best night of her life. They were just going to walk away from it, from each other, no harm, no foul.

Then again, there was no need to prolong an ending that they had both agreed was inevitable. For the first time, though, she had a feeling it was going to hurt like hell to walk away.

"WE HAVE A PROBLEM." The Investor's voice was an annoyed rasp on the other end of the line, sending a shiver down the back of Percy's neck. "Or should I say that *you* have a problem?"

The shiver stayed put even though the thermostat in the mayor's office was set to seventy-eight except when there were eco-lobbyists in the vicinity, which there weren't today. He was still wearing his suit jacket from an earlier on-camera appearance, although he'd lost the tie. And, as he sat at his desk and covered his eyes with one hand to block out the too-bright sunlight coming in through the window, he started to sweat and the smell of his early lunch instantly went from tempting to puke-inducing.

"I did it," he whispered. "Is that what you want to hear? I did it. I went up there and punched holes in the lines myself. I didn't trust anyone else to do it right." Or to stay quiet about it.

He hadn't anticipated the guilt, though, or how he kept seeing the way the steering lines had bled bloody red, glistening in the feeble beam of his penlight after he stabbed them. He smelled the ooze when he closed his eyes, and he'd dreamed of the way it had felt to cut them—initial resistance followed by an easier give once the blade bit through the outer covering of each hose, making incisions small enough that the vehicle would be miles away from Station Fourteen—the last station at the edge of beyond—when it failed.

Guilt, yeah. That was the heavy pressure on his chest that wasn't letting him breathe. He had killed Williams and the woman himself rather than just turning his usual blind eye while his business partner did the dirty work. And he hadn't even had the guts to do it cleanly.

"You did it yourself so it wouldn't get screwed up? That's rich, because guess what? It got screwed up. More accurately, *you* screwed it up. I said to make it look like an accident, not give them every damn option to survive... and come close to blowing my operation right to hell."

Percy's head came up and his hand slapped flat on the desk. *"What?"*

"You heard me," the Investor snarled. "The detective and his little tree doctor survived the crash. What's more, they somehow made it out to the processing site, sneaked into the lab, disabled the DB-Auto and sneaked out again."

"They... Oh, hell." The sweat was flowing in earnest now, making Percy feel oily and desperate.

The Investor gave an inarticulate snarl of fury. When the other man regained his voice, he grated, "What's more, nobody I've talked to knows how to undo what she's done to the DB. It's got some sort of personal code attached to it, and if we don't use the right one, the whole damn system could shut itself down and take the refinement protocol with it."

"Can't you buy another machine and upload the protocol?"

Dead. Silence.

"Oh," Percy said, guessing too late what had happened: namely, that the scientist who had developed the drug must have fouled all the backup material somehow, probably as a way of ensuring his own survival. The researcher, Dr. Ervil Howard, had started out a willing partner, but had balked once he realized the drug was being field tested in Bear Claw. He had disappeared a few months ago, and Percy hadn't asked about him. He'd just taken it as an object lesson in what happened to people who crossed the Investor. Like him.

They survived the crash. The ominous words replayed themselves in his mind, taunting and jeering with the knowledge that although he might have been thinking only moments earlier that he'd give anything to go back and not sabotage the SUV, now all he could think was that he was totally screwed. "I'm sorry. You said to make it look like an accident."

"I said for you to make them go away. You didn't. But as much as I dislike second chances, I'm going to make an exception in this case."

Meaning he wanted Percy to go after them again. Which, if he wound up caught, would be one-hundred-percent political suicide, and in an election year. The mayor's fingers tightened on the phone. "But…"

There was a hesitation before a deadly-sounding "Yes?"

"There's an election coming up, and already rumors

that there's going to be a real candidate this time. That ranger, Matt Blackthorn. He was a poli-sci major, did ten years as a cop and another eight as a ranger. He's perfect for the job." Not to mention perfectly upstanding. If he got even a whiff of how fast and loose the mayor had been playing with city finances, Percy wouldn't just lose the election, he'd also stand a good chance of landing in jail. "I can't do this right now. I just can't." Surely the man on the other end of the phone would understand? The mayor's office was one of his investments, after all. "Can't you just...take care of them?"

"I've done entirely too much of that over the years, which is why we both find ourselves in the current predicament." The Investor paused. "Face it, Proudfoot, both of our tenures in Bear Claw are almost over. At least mine is. For you, it's decision time. You can either man up, take care of this problem you've created, and come with me when I move my operations someplace bigger and better... or you can stay behind."

Quailing at the idea of being stuck in Bear Claw without his investment adviser—mentor, business partner, whatever—Percy locked on to the important part of that. "What do you mean, bigger and better?"

"Exactly what I said. What do you want to be next, a member of the state senate? A congressman? More? If you do this for me, if you commit yourself to me fully, I can make that happen. You'll be an important man, a successful one. Doors will open, women will throw themselves at you, men will want what you have."

The sweat was trickling down Percy's spine now, simultaneously hot and cold as he alternated between horror and excitement. But what choice did he have, really? He had committed himself to the devil years ago; it was far too late to turn back now and they both knew it.

He took a long look around the glossy office, noticing for the first time in a while that the woodwork was stained pine, the gloss a couple of layers of polyurethane. "Okay, I'll... Okay. Whatever you want. Just take me with you."

"Good. You've made a wise choice, Mr. Mayor. Now, here's what I need you to do..."

Chapter Thirteen

"You're sure you're okay?" Chondra's eyes radiated concern from the computer screen. Behind her, thanks to the uplink's clarity, Tori could make out the organized chaos of desks and the black borders of several motivational posters—and one joke demotivational one—about working hard and saving the environment.

Normally, Tori didn't much care where she was as long as the work was interesting and she was making progress, and maybe having a little fun during her downtime. Now, though, she found herself wishing she were back in the lab, separated from the rest of the world by a layer of academia. She and Jack had gotten back to Bear Claw City mid-morning, and he'd almost immediately been whisked off by his boss, Tucker McDermott. Jack had looked back at her and sketched a wave as he was being hauled off, and she couldn't stop wondering if he'd been trying to say he'd see her later, or goodbye, or what.

Not that she was going to tell Chondra that because she would know that the situation had to be really bad for Tori to be stressing over a guy. Her friend would see it as a sign that she was transferring her other fears on to something that usually wouldn't matter to her, and maybe she would be right.

Because she wanted her friends to worry less, not more, Tori gave an "everything's cool" shrug and said, "I'm perfectly safe. I'm working out of the city's crime lab, which is in the basement of the main P.D."

It was a well-appointed basement, she thought with a quick look around at the computer space of the multi-room lab space, which had top-notch if slightly dated equipment, well-organized workstations and cheerful artwork on the walls. It was still a basement, though, and she was the only one down there, and had been for most of the day.

The crime scene analysts—all high-powered, self-confident women—had been in and out when she first arrived, showing her around and offering her any help she needed as she continued to analyze the fungus, not only looking for a way to cure the forest now, but also a way to treat the Death Stare addiction, maybe even prevent death in the case of an overdose. The analysts had been friendly and welcoming, and had made the lab come alive. As the morning wore on, though, and the department mobilized to work the new connections Tori and Jack had discovered, the others had disappeared, leaving her alone.

Chondra's lips pursed. "I'm glad they've got you under lock and key, but it's not what I was asking about. What's wrong?"

The good news, Tori thought, was that she was back down in Bear Claw with access to a real network and functional uplink. The bad news was that she was back in Bear Claw with access to a real network and functional uplink...because the speed and clarity of the data feed not only gave her access to all the databases and files she needed, it also made it impossible for her to dodge her friend's concern with excuses about bad connections and fuzzy video.

She started to brush it off, but the honest worry in her friend's expression had her sighing instead. "I'll be fine, I promise. And I appreciate your concern, but…not now, okay? Right now I'd really like to focus on the work. We can catch up on the other stuff later." As in way later, once she'd gotten some distance in time and space, and with it, some perspective. "How are you doing on figuring where this thing came from?"

Chondra hesitated momentarily, as if to say *I know you're changing the subject, and I'm going to let you get away with it, but only for now.* But then her eyes took on a triumphant glitter. "We got it."

"You got it." Tori closed her eyes and breathed a "Thank you," then opened her eyes, feeling her spirits start to lift. "Talk to me."

"Meet Dr. Erwin Howard." Chondra clicked her mouse a few times, and a small window popped up in the corner of the video screen. It showed a mug shot–type ID photo of a middle-aged guy wearing glasses and showing a lot of teeth. "He was a tenured prof at one of the big universities in North Carolina, with a big lab and some serious grant money behind him, both private and federal. As you figured, he was working on bioengineering an organism that could be used to pull dispersed metals—either contamination or natural reserves—out of large patches of soil. Actually, the fungus was part of a symbiotic process, paired up with a fast-growing, deep-rooting plant that did the actual mining, with the fungus concentrating the metal for harvesting."

"I vaguely remember the project, but it seemed like it

petered out after a while." Or folded up entirely, Tori realized. "You keep saying 'was'…what happened to him?" Unfortunately, she had a pretty good guess.

"He disappeared a little over two years ago, along with copies of his notes and samples of all his work. At the time, everyone thought he would turn up working for one of the really cutting-edge metal-refining companies. He never did, though."

The confirmation put a queasy shiver down the back of her neck. The shimmies only got worse when she combined that with the abandoned-looking workstation and the fact that the last programming in the DB-Auto had been time-stamped several months earlier. Granted, Dr. Howard might have moved on from the mobile lab setup, or been paid off and gone on to spend his ill-gotten gains. She had a feeling, though, that wasn't the way the militia worked, and that the scientist might very well be dead.

She rubbed her hands over her arms reflexively, shivering even though it was comfortably warm in the basement lab. The move made her very aware of the echoing emptiness of the lab space, though, and the nerves just served to reinforce the knowledge that she was seriously off balance, off her game. She didn't feel like herself, didn't even look like herself really.

She had gotten a change of clothes from one of the CSIs—a dark-haired profiler named Maya Thorne. The other woman was petite enough that at least Tori wasn't swimming in the borrowed clothes, but the other woman's high-end, understated taste was very different from Tori's usual preference. The tailored navy slacks and silky, subtly ruffled button-down shirt were loose on her but still managed to feel constricting somehow…and the navy-

and-yellow "Property of the BCCPD" sweatshirt Tori was wearing for warmth, which Maya had scrounged from another of the CSI's lockers, held a good dose of irony after last night.

Don't go there.

"Are you getting anywhere with an antidote?" Chondra asked, bringing her back on task.

Tori gave herself a mental shake and, when she realized she had spun around in her chair so she was facing the doorway leading to the main stairs rather than her borrowed workstation, she deliberately turned around and put her back to the door. The floor above her was crawling with cops, so there was no way the militia could get to her, and she didn't need company, darn it. She was fine on her own.

Aware that her friend would have seen the carousel routine and had to be wondering about it, Tori cleared her throat, tapped a few keys to zip several files into an emailable package, and sent it to Chondra's address. "I'm sending you what we've come up with so far." Although Tori and her lab employees weren't drug specialists by a long shot, the FBI analysts who had taken over that part of the investigation had asked her to stay on the case from her end, knowing she might have a unique take on things. "A couple of labs in this country and a few more abroad have been working on using the parental fungus for medical applications."

"I thought it was poisonous."

"There are dozens of compounds out there that are medicinal at one dose, poisonous at another, higher dose," Tori pointed out, trying not to sound like an instant expert after several hours spent reading up on the three organisms that had been spliced together to create her, or rather Bear Claw's, fungus.

"True enough." Chondra's attention went to the corner of her screen, then returned to Tori. "Your email just came through. What do you want me to look for?"

"Have you been able to get in touch with anyone from Howard's old lab?"

"I've got a friend in the department, actually. She's getting us everything she can find and will email what she can and ship the rest."

"If it hasn't already shipped, have her hold on to it. I have a feeling it should go straight to the task force, do not pass go, do not collect two hundred. I'll check on that, though." Tori wrote herself a reminder, then said, "Beyond that, just keep doing what you've been doing all along."

"Except that now I can do it officially."

"There is that." The moment Tori's bosses at the university and in the Park Service had heard about her discovery, they had thrown their full support back behind the investigation. Which probably should have been gratifying rather than annoying, but she figured she was entitled to a little grouchiness given that they hadn't trusted her word in the first place. Granted, they'd had a point about the danger. But if she hadn't stayed, they wouldn't be where they were right now with the case.

Or her emotions, for that matter, although that hadn't been the danger her bosses had been worried about.

Don't think about it.

"Given that the task force seems to be more focused on the Death Stare drug angle, do you want me to concentrate on ways we might be able to help the forest?"

"No, I'd like you to take a look at what they've come

up with for antidotes against the addictions and over-doses, and see if you see something they haven't thought of. People are dying, and that's got to take precedence over the forest." When guilt stung, Tori added defensively, "It's the right thing to do."

"I know that…I just didn't think you did." Chondra's expression went speculative. "And no offense, because you know I love you just the way you are, but I'm not sure you would have put drug users over the possible demise of a state park last week. So what gives?" Her eyes sparked. "Did something happen between you and the hunky cop bodyguard you were telling me about?" Whatever she saw in Tori's expression must have given it away because her mouth went round in an O of surprise and excitement. "It did! Come on, come on, give me something here. Remember that I'm stuck back here in the lab, living my dreams of adventure vicariously through you."

Tori snorted. "Your idea of an adventure is sidewalk sale day at the outlet mall, not roughing it overnight in a cave."

"A cave? Sounds romantic. And potentially Freudian."

That surprised a rusty laugh out of Tori, but she shook her head. "It was…" She trailed off because it hadn't been perfect, not by a long shot, but that was the word that kept getting stuck in her head. That wasn't right, though, it couldn't be.

Could it?

You're just tired, stressed out, strung out, she told her-self. There was no other reason why she would be so close to tears for no reason.

Chondra's smile tipped to real concern. "Seriously, Tori. Are you okay?"

To her surprise, she was sorely tempted to talk it out when that had never been her thing before. To her, guys came and went. Sometimes it pinched, sometimes it was a relief, and most times it was with fond memories and promises of "I'll see you around." Now, though, she was worked up, churned up, her emotions far too close to the surface of her mind.

Knowing that she didn't dare let any of that loose, though—not now, when she needed to be focusing on the case and handling herself in as professional a manner as possible—she shook her head and swallowed down the choking emotions to say, "Listen, we'll talk about it later, okay? Much later."

Chondra looked dubious. "Okay, but if you change your mind…"

"I won't."

"If you do, call me, anytime. I mean it."

Tori nodded, but didn't quite trust herself to speak.

"And do me a favor? Give this guy a chance. If he's got you all worked up like this, he's got real potential."

"I'm worried about the investigation, not him," Tori contradicted, hearing the edge of desperation in her own voice. "He doesn't figure into this. If anything, I'm worked up because I'm itching to get out of here. With the feds on the case and things moving in the directions of biochemistry and genetic engineering rather than plant pathology, I'm not really needed." The statement brought a dull ache that served only to increase her growing conviction that she'd be better off hitting the road sooner than later.

"But your detective—"

"He's not my detective," Tori interrupted too sharply, then sighed and shook her head. "Sorry. I just…I need to get out of here, that's all." She reached for the cutoff. "I'll call you later, okay?"

Chondra had barely begun a too-perceptive, too-sympathetic nod when Tori killed the feed. Then she just sat there for a long moment, staring at the computer screen, which showed her email in-box. It was loaded with everything from routine correspondence to flagged answers to her inquiries on the Bear Claw case. And although she knew she had to keep going, she couldn't make herself click on the first of those flagged messages.

She didn't want to think about the case right now, which was selfish, just as it had been selfish of her to hang up on Chondra when she was only trying to help. And even that selfishness wasn't typical of her—usually she turned her moods inward, hiding them from others and dealing with them in private. Not now, though. Now, she was stirred up…and none of that mattered. What mattered was that there was a chance that she could help the task force find a treatment for the fungal poisoning, and save some lives in the process. Which had to trump anything she might, or might not, have going on in her personal life.

Tapping her forehead against her closed fist, she said, "You've gotta pull it together and figure out where to go from here."

"I hear Maine is nice this time of year," Jack said from behind her.

She stiffened, heart leaping at the sound of his voice. "Jack!" She turned her chair to find him standing in the doorway, filling it with the sheer impact he commanded in clean jeans, a tight white T-shirt, shoulder holster and leather jacket. But any thought she might have had that he was suggesting a romantic getaway died the instant she saw his thunderous expression. She lowered the hand she had started to hold out to him. "Jack?"

He narrowed his eyes. "If you want to go, then just go. Nobody's stopping you."

Shock slapped through her, driving her to her feet to face him. That shock should have been followed quickly by anger, which was her usual fallback response when faced with irrationality, especially in the form of someone so much larger than her. Her hands should have balled to fists and she should have given him a "What the hell?" or some version of it.

There was nothing usual about today, though, and there was nothing typical about the way her throat closed in hurt and dismay as he straightened away from the door-frame and crossed to her, not stopping until they stood toe to toe. He stared down at her, mouth tight, eyes as cold as if those deep lakes had frozen over to glaciers that had no hope of a thaw for a long, long time.

She started to reach for him, but the downward twitch of his mouth stopped her, as did the sure knowledge that he didn't want her touching him now.

"Wait, why are you…" she began, but then trailed off as she remembered the things she'd said to get Chondra off her back when it came to him. *He doesn't figure into this,* she had said. And was there anything more dismissive than that? She had also denied that he was her detective—even though that was how she'd been thinking of him for far too long—and she'd said she needed to get out of there. She had meant the basement, not the city, though she could certainly understand how he could make the leap given his own personal history. "Jack, wait. Listen. I didn't mean—"

"Stop," he said sharply. "Think about it, because whatever you say next had damn well better be the truth."

Again, her normal response would have been anger. Again, she felt pain instead. More, she imagined his pain, as well. She hated that he'd heard the things she'd said, wished she could go back and delete them because she would have hated to hear them if the roles had been reversed. Because of that, she breathed past her instinctive and indignant denial, and said firmly, "I have *never* lied to you. Not once."

"Last night you asked me to make love to you," he rasped. And for a second, she thought she saw pain behind the anger as he said, "Sex is just sex. Making love is the next step in a relationship, even one in fast-forward like ours."

Thudda-thudda went her heart, and she blew out a soft "Oh" of understanding. "Jack, no…" she began, and reached up to touch his face as she had done time and again throughout the night until it had become in a way her own private code for "It's you, you're really here," which had come to matter to her more and more as the night had gone on, though not as much as he had apparently thought.

Now, however, he flinched and backed up a step, then glared at her, and the expression immediately did away with any thought she might have had that he was in pain. The only thing she could see in him right then was a familiar sort of cold, hard judgment—the kind that said he was a cop and that meant he knew the truth of the matter, even if he didn't really.

It also said that she had imagined the pain she had seen, or if she'd seen the flinch for real, it had been a momentary thing. Because guys who looked at their lovers—their wives, their children—like that weren't the kind of guys to worry about pain. That was how they lost their lovers, wives and children, after all.

Watch the baggage, she warned herself, well aware that he'd proven to her before that he wasn't exactly like the others, even if right now he looked far more like one of them than was comfortable for her. But she was also well aware that he could have a point, whether she liked it or not.

"I don't see making love as being the same thing as making a promise or commitment," she said, trying to choose her words so it didn't sound like she was devaluing his way of looking at things, or her own. "To me, it's expressing the joy of liking the other person, being attracted to them, and making a mutual decision to enjoy each other's bodies." She paused, and when he didn't say anything, just kept staring at her with that cold, cold look in his eyes, she said softly, "I never said anything about a relationship or a future, Jack. In fact, I was very clear two nights ago that I wasn't looking for those things." Why did saying that make her feel like something was tearing apart inside her when it was the truth? She continued on, though. "You were the one who said you'd had a revelation back at the encampment, that you'd changed your mind about things."

"Yeah, I decided that maybe it was possible for me to fall for someone in the space of a few days, and that my feelings weren't any less important just because they grew up so damned fast." He barked a bitter laugh. "Guess I was wrong about that one."

"I'm sorry, Jack," she said on a sigh that threatened to

crack as she started to realize that they'd had two totally different experiences the night before. How could they have been so exquisitely connected on every other level, and so far apart on this one?

Moreover, deep down inside, nerves were starting to stir when it connected that what she'd been feeling from him—the intensity, the passion—had been the beginnings of what he would bring to a relationship. That wasn't the scary part, though, because it had been magnificent. The truly terrifying thing was that she knew there was an ultimatum coming, and that it would be one she couldn't live with, not even to get that kind of loving. Which would mean walking away from it—away from *him*—instead, and the thought of it tore her up inside.

"Don't say you're sorry. Say you'll stay for a while and see if there's a chance for us together." And, damn it, his expression softened and she saw the pain again.

I don't do "together" she thought as panic lumped in her throat. She didn't say it aloud, though, because the panic wasn't entirely coming from the fact that he was caging her in and forcing her to make a choice. Some of it—most of it—was coming from the fact that she was, for the first time in her life, tempted to say yes.

Yes, I'll stay, she wanted to say. *Yes, I'll give it a try.* Heck, she would do better than try because she could do almost anything if she put her mind to it…and that was part of what terrified her, because if she set it as her goal to stay with Jack, make things work with him, what would she be giving up to succeed? She could just see herself getting lost in a life she hadn't chosen, hadn't wanted. Unless…

She took a breath, couldn't believe she was going to

say it, but said it anyway. "How about you come with me instead? Not for long. Just for a few days, a week or so, and see how it goes?" The tentative, ineloquent offer made her once again feel awkward and out of her depth. In this case, though, she didn't mind as much. This was a first for her, after all, and when she found herself holding her breath and searching his face for an answer, she realized it was something she wanted very, very badly indeed. She wanted to make love with him again, repeatedly, wanted to show him her world and expand the limits of his own.

And maybe that meant she had the potential to do "together," or at least try it, with him.

It was only a three-count, maybe less, before he shook his head and his expression fell into one of a cop's regret, the one that said, "Ma'am, I have bad news for you…"

"Tori—" he began, but stopped when she held up her hand.

"Never mind. I know you've got your life here, your career, this case…I don't blame you. Really I don't." How could she? She was a bad risk on the relationship front, and she was offering him a lifestyle he didn't want.

He cleared his throat, not looking cold now so much as fatally resigned. "If you won't stay and I won't go, then where does that leave us?"

"Working different ends of the same case," she said, going for a chirpy tone that she suspected fell badly short of the mark. "Which is what I should probably be getting back to, if we're done here."

She didn't wait for his response, just spun in her chair and hit the keys to pull up the first of the flagged emails. And as she stared at it, she did her damnedest not to sniffle, wipe her face or give any other indication of the tears that had gathered and broken free.

Just go, she urged him silently. *Stay mad at me and go.* Because if he saw she was crying he would know she wasn't nearly so convinced as she needed to be. And if he said anything to soothe her, she would lose it. Either way, he would know just how vulnerable she was to him right now, and that if he pushed hard enough, he might get her to agree to something that she didn't want to do.

Knowing that was almost as terrifying as walking across the militia encampment in a dead man's hat and shirt, hoping to hell nobody noticed her.

After a moment, his footsteps moved away. She heard him cross the room and head back up the stairs, leaving her sitting alone, trying to make sense of the computer screen as she swiped away her tears.

"Damn it." She hated crying, hated that she'd hurt him and let herself be hurt in return. Of course he wasn't going to come with her; that hadn't ever been on the table. For a moment there, though, she had dared to hope. And even that much had been too much. "Damn, damn, damn."

She scrubbed at her face with her sleeve, thankful for the first time that she was entirely alone in the lab, because there was nobody there to see her struggling to pull it back together. She was there to do a job, period, end of story. And it was time to get back to work.

But when she heard a set of men's footsteps coming down the stairs, her heart didn't just give a *thudda-thudda,* it took up the whole percussion line of a decent dance number, rocking and rolling in her chest as she turned slowly in her chair, trying not to look desperate as she said, "I'm glad you— Oh, I'm sorry. I thought you were someone else."

"I get that a lot," the stranger said, grinning as he hit the bottom of the stairs and came through the door to the lab's data-crunching area where she'd set up shop. "Tori Bay, right?" As he got within a few strides of her, he held out a hand. "I'm Percy."

He was of average height, build and looks, with thinning mid-brown hair, murky eyes and decent business casual going on in the clothing department.

Her pulse sagged back to normal as she rose and shook. "As in, Mayor Percy Proudfoot?" His hand was dry and a little cool, and even up close she couldn't really get his face imprinted on her mind. She had a feeling that five minutes after they parted, she wouldn't be able to pick him out of a lineup if her life had depended on it.

His grin almost made dimples. "That's me. I'd ask for your vote, but I understand you're not from around here."

"Just passing through," she said, not quite able to suppress the pang. She thought it prudent not to mention that he would have been hard pressed to get her vote anyway, given that he'd cut the P.D.'s budget to the bone during the course of his first term. In fact, she was surprised to find him nonthreatening, with an open, earnest face that inclined her to like him right off the bat.

Then again, he was a politician.

"What can I do for you?" she asked as she reclaimed her hand. Turning, she gestured to the computer. "Want me to run you through what we've got so far on the Death Stare investigation?"

"No, thanks, I'm up to date on that. I actually came to get you for an appointment across town."

"Excuse me?" She glanced back over her shoulder at him. "I think there's been a—"

He was suddenly right beside her, crowding her as he got one arm around her shoulder and his hand across her mouth, then used the other to deliver a painful jab in her kidney that had her sagging against him with a muffled, disbelieving cry.

No!

Her heart hammered suddenly in her ears and adrenaline flared in a wild surge. She stumbled back and tried to yank away from him, but he torqued her shoulder and jabbed her again, this time in the side, growling, "Quit it. See that?" He wrenched her head down, forcing her to look at the gun he had partway buried in her borrowed sweatshirt.

She moaned at the sight of a snub-nosed .38. The little gun didn't have much power, but at close range it would do some serious damage.

"Right. Behave and it doesn't go off. Screw with me and it does. Got it?"

Rolling her eyes in an effort to see her captor, near panic as she struggled to breathe through nasal passages gone tight from her recent tears, she nodded jerkily, tried to speak but couldn't, and wound up whimpering instead—a sad, pitiful noise that said *Why?*

"I need your help with a project," he said, all of a sudden sounding eerily calm, as if the two of them were negotiating for a dozen more picnic tables on the common. "But first things first, we need to get out of here without attracting any real attention. So we're going to walk nice and easy. You're going to speak when spoken to, and do whatever it takes to get us out of here. If you don't, I'll shoot you and then I'll shoot whoever you were talking to. And I'll keep shooting until I get clear of the building. Any questions?"

The horrible scene painted itself so vividly in her mind that she could picture the blood, hear the screams, and had to do her best not to put faces to the images. She shuddered and shook her head in a violent negative.

"You'll behave?"

A nod. *Yes.*

In a flash, his hand was off her mouth, his grip shifted so it looked like they were walking together like new friends who'd hit it off right away. "Move," he directed tersely. "Out the back and up to the parking lot. And don't try anything."

"I won't," she whispered, her voice gone thin and shaky with a terrible fear that grew as he used an official code to get them through a rear exit that she'd been told was completely sealed off. No doubt that was how he'd gotten into the building in the first place. Things got even worse when he hustled her over to a white Cadillac parked at the farthest extent of the lot, just out of range of the security cameras, and popped the trunk. She balked. "No!"

Her struggles didn't matter, though; he was stronger and ruthless, and used his fierce grip on her arm to lever her into the cavernous trunk, which smelled of spare tire and spilled cherry soda. Once she was in there, he held the gun on her, pulled a bungee cord from a dark, dank corner and said, "Hold out your hands."

Feeling smaller and weaker than she had in years, maybe ever, she did as she was told, then flinched when he whipped the elastic cord around her wrists and then latched the curved ends together. "It's too tight," she said, voice breaking. "My hands are going numb."

"I don't give a… Damn it." He loosened the cord one turn and refastened it. Then he leaned in and gave her a thorough but impersonal pat-down, finding nothing because she was wearing borrowed clothes and had her own stuff in her knapsack back at the lab. Grimacing, he shot her a narrow-eyed glare. "Remember, you do anything to draw attention, and you're going to be responsible for the deaths of anyone who comes after you."

She nodded miserably, and then screamed involuntarily when he slammed the trunk. The noise was very loud, very final, and it left her alone in the darkness knowing one thing for certain: unless she thought fast and managed to do something to save herself, she wasn't ever going to get a chance to tell Jack that she was sorry for what she'd said to Chondra, and that she hadn't meant it. She had been scared of her feelings, scared of what they might mean and what kind of trouble they could get her into.

Now, though, she knew what it felt like to be really, truly scared for her life. And it was very different from the way he made her feel…so different, in fact, that she thought he might make her feel something other than fear, after all. She wasn't ready to give it a name yet, but as the vehicle bumped its way down from the elevated parking area and the mayor accelerated away, taking her God only knew where, she whispered deep in her heart, *Please, Jack, trust me. Trust us. And please don't think I left without saying goodbye.*

Chapter Fourteen

On his way back to the task force's war room after his run-in with Tori, Jack got waylaid by two guys with legit questions about the vehicles and arms he'd seen at the encampment, and two others who could have answered their own damn questions if they'd just read the transcripts of his and Tori's debriefings. Finally free of them, and without having caused major bloodshed, he decided on a detour to the vending machines. Like a soda was going to fix things.

But as he passed a cracked-open door, a voice called, "Hey, Jack. Got a second?"

He had turned with a snarl before it registered: Tucker's door, Tucker's voice. He exhaled and made an effort to smooth out as he strode through the door.

Tucker must have seen his first reaction, though, because he waved to the visitor's chair. "Sit. Talk to me." And when Jack made an "it's nothing" gesture, he pointed to the chair. "I said sit. The last time you got this wound tight, my witness ended up in the E.R. Not your fault directly, granted, but I know you. If you'd been on your game, that guy never would have gone down."

"Hell." Jack sat. "Yeah, you're right about that." At Tucker's surprised look, he shrugged. "You told me to use my time in the woods to do some thinking. Mission accomplished. I won't be doing Ray any favors by going off half-cocked or screwing up perfectly good police work, and I'm sure as hell not interested in helping out the members of the Shadow Militia by giving their eventual lawyers something to work with on getting them off." He nodded. "I'm good. I'm solid. You don't need to worry about me."

Tucker regarded him for a long moment, then nodded. "Okay, I'll buy that. So what was the snarl for? Someone hassling you?"

Jack intended to brush him off with a vague reference to the two idiots who had decided to waste time tracking him down and quizzing him rather than reading the damn transcript—or, hell, asking someone who had read it. Somehow, though, the words got all turned around in his brain, and what he wound up saying was, "How is it that two rational, intelligent adults could have entire conversations where they end up agreeing with each other, but it later turns out that they thought they agreed to two completely different things?"

Tucker blinked. Then the corner of his mouth twitched. "Welcome to the world of adult relationships."

"I'm being serious here."

"So am I." Glancing at the framed photo of his wife and daughter, as if wary on some level that they could hear him, he said, "Look, men and women are wired differently, so sometimes they're just not going to process the same information in the same way. Add in some preconceptions and the basic human desire to get our own way if it isn't going to hurt anyone else, and you've got the potential to do some major talking past each other."

Jack frowned and shook his head. "Kayla and I never did that."

"Or else you did and neither of you ever figured it out. Which might be part of why it didn't work. You weren't pushing hard enough to get to the bottom of things."

"We…" Jack's brain stuttered to a halt. "What?"

"I take it you and Tori had a fight?" Tucker shrugged. "Well, fights happen in every relationship, sometimes more so when you're off to a quick start like the two of you seem to be."

Still trying to catch up with Tucker's offhand comment about him and Kayla, Jack said, "Yes. No. Hell, I don't know. For starters, we're not in a relationship, which was news to me." Without really meaning to, he gave his boss a five-minute rundown of his and Tori's interactions, which to him had been a romance, to her a good time. He kept it tame, knowing that Tucker would fill in the blanks as needed, and ended with, "I don't know, maybe she's right. Why make ourselves crazy trying to make it work?"

Tucker just shot him this smug Cheshire cat grin and said, "Because when it works, it's the best damn thing in the universe." He tapped the picture frame. "I wasn't looking for this when I came here, but I found it, and I worked for it and made the changes I needed to make. We both did, and I'm damned grateful for that—for them— every single day. Alyssa made my life better and the baby made us a family. That's the golden ring, Jack, at least it turned out to be for me. And I think it's even more that way for you. You're a domesticated kind of guy, a family man. You deserve that…but it's not going to just show up on your doorstep, and it might not even show up when, how and looking like you want it to." Tucker paused and looked from the photo back to Jack. "I don't know if she's the one for you, buddy, but she's sure as hell the most interesting candidate since I've known you. You're fired up like I've never seen you before, and that's not just the way the case is breaking. It's her, and the two of you together. There's something there, and I think you should ask yourself whether, if you let her go now, you're going to kick yourself bloody later."

Head spinning, Jack said, "You're saying I should... what? Offer to go with her? Try to talk her into staying here? Do the long-distance thing?"

"None of that matters really until you're sure she's the one and vice versa. And I predict that when you've gotten to know her a bit better, and you're sure she's it for you, then the other stuff isn't going to seem nearly so important. This isn't real estate, Jack, with all the 'location, location, location' crap. This is romance, and it's about the two of you and whether you care enough about each other to make it work."

"But the things she said to her friend..."

"Could have been Tori's way of saying she didn't want to talk about it...or maybe she wants to mean it because of the way she's been living her life. Because from the looks of you two together this morning, you're probably not the only one who's doing some reevaluating and not finding it all that comfortable a process." Tucker paused, then grinned. "But like I said, when it's right, it's so damn worth it." And this time when he went for his drawer, he bypassed the antacids and went for an energy bar instead, as if to say *It's the job that runs me ragged; being a husband and father is the good part.*

"You know," Jack said reflectively after a moment, "I

think that's the most I've ever heard you say about anything ever." When Tucker's eyes kindled, he held up a hand. "And no, that's not all I got out of it. I got a hell of a lot out of it, in fact, so thanks. I appreciate it."

"And you're going to go back down and talk to her?"

Jack glanced in the direction of the vending machines and the task force's war room, then the opposite way, to the stairs leading down. "Yeah, I'm going to try, anyway. The whole talking past each other thing has me a little on edge."

"Mars. Venus. It happens. If this thing is going to happen between you two, you'll work it out. If not, well, it's good exercise for the next time around."

When Jack's gut tightened at how casually Tucker was throwing around the idea of a "next time," he was forced to admit—inwardly, at least—that he was already a fair ways down the long slide of falling for Tori. Which was probably why it had ripped him up so badly to hear her dismiss him like that to her friend, and why he'd pushed things further than he probably should have with her.

Well, she'd had some time to take a breath—they both had. Maybe it was time for round two. "The task force is meeting in fifteen," he said with a nod. "I'll see you in there."

The corners of Tucker's eyes crinkled. "Good luck."

"Thanks, I'm gonna—" He broke off at a shout from out in the hallway, which was followed by a volley of questions, and then more shouts, unintelligible but urgent. "What the hell?"

Jack spun for the door as Tucker got up and moving, and both of their phones started going off simultaneously. The yelling got louder, the ringing kept up and things were teetering on the brink of chaos when Tucker tossed his phone to Jack with a terse "Take this," and stepped out into the hallway to bellow, "Quiet!"

The bull pen went dead silent. Even the on-loaner feds clammed up, although they made it look like they were just playing along. The phones stopped ringing, dumping to voice mail.

Pointing at a grizzled veteran who still wore his uniform because he'd had no interest in being promoted to soft clothes, Tucker said, "Twenty words or less. What the hell is going on?"

"The prints came back from the brake and steering lines of Detective Williams's car, sir. He didn't even wear gloves, cocky bastard." The sneer in his voice made it sound personal.

"Who did the prints ping to?" Tucker prodded.

It was Jack, in the middle of checking their voice mails, who cursed and said, "It was Proudfoot."

Tucker whipped around. "The mayor? Seriously?" But he was more surprised than disbelieving. He, like most of the others, was plenty ready to pin something on the slick bastard.

That it had turned out to be this big…well, yeah, that was a hell of a surprise.

"Son of a bitch," Jack muttered under his breath as it started to sink in. "The bastard tried to kill me and Tori personally. Why, because we were getting too close to the drug operations? Is that why he's been making it so damned difficult to get choppers and supplies up to the Forgotten?" All of a sudden, a bunch of things that had seemed like old-fashioned penny-pinching started to seem more like part of a larger, more insidious whole.

"War room, now," Tucker snapped, waving them all in that direction. As an aside to Jack, he said, "Sorry, you're going to have to postpone the semi-groveling."

"Duty calls." And there was no way he was missing out on this takedown, especially knowing that Tori was safely tucked away downstairs, with a whole layer of cops between her and their enemy...aka one Percy Proudfoot, slimeball mayor of Bear Claw City.

The task force meeting was brief, mostly because they couldn't afford to give any leaks time to warn the mayor. Although the information flow had been kept as tight as possible, there was always the risk, especially when politics were involved. The plan was simple: lock down the mayor's office, his mansion and the private residence he'd kept hold of when he moved into the mansion. The warrants were being issued, the evidence being lined up and vetted by the prosecutors. The moment the task force had the go-ahead, they were moving in.

That meant, though, that Jack had a few minutes before he needed to be rolling. As he headed for the door, he caught Tucker's eye and got a nod, along with a gesture that he thought meant *Good luck.* Or maybe it was more along the lines of *Don't get too caught up in the little stuff when the big picture works so damn well,* which was what he was starting to tell himself. Because Tucker was right: if he and Tori worked together as a couple—and it sure as hell seemed like they did—then they could make the other stuff happen, one way or another.

That was a big "if," though. Because despite Tucker's optimism that she, too, had been in mid-freakout over how fast things were moving, she'd been pretty damn clear that she had been in it for the fun. So the question was, had that been a defense mechanism or was that really the way she felt?

He was about to find out.

"It's me," he called as he hit the bottom step. "We need to talk." Then he stopped dead, his stomach sinking as his instincts warned him that he was alone in the basement lab. Still, though, he called, "Tori? You in here?" and did a quick walk-through to be sure.

With each empty room, though, a hollow pressure built in his chest, because those same instincts said she hadn't been upstairs. He would have seen her if she had been. Moreover, his gut said she was all the way gone.

The realization filled him with a turbid mix of emotions. Disbelief, dismay, resentment, betrayal, grief…all of them mixed and mashed together until they formed the inevitable one-two punch of conclusion: one, he was too late to stop her from leaving. And two, she hadn't wanted him enough to stay.

"Damn it," he said softly, not sure which of them he was madder at just then—himself for not pushing harder when he'd had the chance, or her for not pushing at all. Not that it really mattered right then—she was undoubtedly headed for the airport under police escort, although he would double-check to make sure she hadn't gone off on her own. Either way, she was back on the road, he was back on the Death Stare case and the task force was about to move out and go after their primary suspect. Maybe things had turned out the way they were meant to, after all.

"Forget that," he muttered under his breath, and pivoted on his heel. He didn't know what he was going to do, but he knew one thing for sure: he wasn't ready for them to be over. Not by a long shot.

He was halfway across the room when he saw what should have been obvious to his detective self from the very first moment—namely that she'd left her knapsack behind.

And Tori would never, ever leave her knapsack behind.

Blood running suddenly cold in his veins, he back-tracked to the computer station where she'd been sitting. That was definitely her knapsack, and when he tapped the mouse to awaken the computer she'd been using, her email was still open on the main screen. He scanned quickly, didn't see anything that jumped out at him as being a reason for her to take off without her stuff. And yet... Digging into his pocket for the small flashlight he carried there, he clicked on the light and shined it at an oblique angle onto the waxed lab floor.

There were scuff marks. Lots of them. All right near where she'd been sitting.

"Damn it," he grated, gut knotting on a surge of self-directed bile as the worst-case scenario—that she'd been taken—suddenly got way more plausible. "You rotten... Tucker!" he bellowed up the stairs, already moving in that direction. "We've got—" His phone rang, interrupting him.

Thinking it was Tucker calling to tell him that she'd been spotted or, better yet, brought back in safely, he flipped open the phone and said tersely, "This is Williams."

"Jack?" The one small word, a single syllable uttered in a trembling version of Tori's usual sass, nearly brought him to his knees.

Heart thudding double time, he clutched the phone and rasped, "*Tori,* baby, are you okay? Where are you? How did you—"

"No questions," a man's voice broke in, clipped and no-nonsense. "That's rule number one. Rule number two is that you don't let on, not even with a twitch, that you're talking to me. If I see your people anywhere near me between now and when I get what I want, then the woman dies."

"Proudfoot." Jack said the name like a curse.

Ignoring the ID, the mayor said, "Just do what you're told and nobody will get hurt."

"I don't believe that any more than I did your campaign speeches."

"Then lucky for me I've got the leverage."

Damn it. Jack's pulse hammered thickly in his ears and he was suddenly very aware of the thudding boom of footsteps overhead, as the task force started to move out. Although the forward scouts had no doubt already reported that the mayor wasn't at home or the office—there was no way the bastard would make things that easy, he was slippery, not stupid—the warrants could be served, the searches conducted, a BOLO issued…none of which would do Tori any good.

Maybe *he* could, though.

"What do you want?" he said coldly, grimly.

"Meet me at the old deli packaging plant in the warehouse district. You know the one I mean?"

"Yeah, I know it." Jack's mind raced as the activity overhead increased and he imagined Tucker up there, checking the time and wondering where the hell he was. Pretty soon, he'd come down into the lab looking for his missing detective, and things would go from bad to worse. "I can be there in fifteen minutes."

"Make it ten or don't bother."

"Wait!" Jack said quickly. "I want to talk to—" But the line had already gone dead. "No!"

"Jack?" Tucker's voice called down the stairs. "Time to go. And I need my phone back."

"Be right there," he called back, heart thudding a sick, urgent rhythm of *Don't tell, don't tell, don't tell, don't tell.*

For a boy who'd been raised practically from birth to be a cop, the idea of deceiving his commanding officer was untenable. But for a man who'd finally found a woman worth fighting for—maybe even worth changing for—the idea of risking her life by going against Proudfoot's orders wasn't an option either.

Trying desperately for a middle ground, he typed a quick text into his phone but didn't send it. Then he put his phone by Tori's knapsack, made a quick detour to the break room where the CSIs left their personal stuff in open lockers, and pocketed the keys to Alyssa's personal vehicle. "You'll get it back in one piece, I promise," he said to the empty room as he imagined Tucker's fiery wife glaring at him for the well-intentioned theft.

And then, staying casual, he strolled upstairs and right out the front of the P.D., much as he had done in the militia encampment. This time, though, his palms were even sweatier and his gut tied even tighter in knots, and the moment he was out of the line of sight of the others, he sprinted for Alyssa's boxy SUV and had the engine cranking in no time flat.

Still, though, he could feel the seconds ticking down, the time running out, and it made him frantic. He hit the gas and sent the vehicle hurtling out of the parking lot just as the SWAT bus rolled in. He caught sight of surprised faces as he zoomed past and swerved onto the main drag, then punched it to just catch the end of a yellow light.

Ignoring the startled honks of protest, he accelerated away, heading for the warehouse district even as the rest of the task force dispersed to the mayor's properties to lie in wait for him.

Jack, though, knew where Proudfoot was. What he didn't know was what it was going to take to bring him down, and how the hell he was going to do it without Tori getting hurt. Because she was his priority now. And, if he got lucky, maybe tomorrow as well, and all the tomorrows after that.

Don't get ahead of yourself, he cautioned. And edging the gas pedal even closer to the floor, he sent the SUV flying through the city, feeling like he was back on his home territory, and ready to kick ass, take names and punish the bastard who'd raped the city's coffers, exposed its citizens to a poisonous drug and dared to touch his woman.

Proudfoot was doomed. He just didn't know it yet.

Chapter Fifteen

"Do it," Proudfoot growled, pressing the sharp needle tip of a filled syringe against the side of Tori's neck like a metal caress. "Unlock the damn machine and I'll let you go."

She couldn't stop the whimper, couldn't control the slamming of her heart, couldn't find the confident, sassy woman who'd learned to handle herself over the years.

Then again, she'd never had to handle anything like this before.

She had never in her life hated being pint-size as much as she did right now. Logic said that even a stronger, taller woman would have had trouble with Proudfoot armed and completely uncaring of her pain. But it was still demeaning to be so thoroughly overpowered. Her skin throbbed with bruises from her futile struggles, and her wrists stung from where the bungee had rubbed her raw. He'd taken off the cord, but it lay nearby, coiled like a nylon snake. She was sick and shaking, impotent. And she hated it, hated him.

He was leaning over her, practically on top of her as she sat at the console of the DB-Auto she'd fried the day before. His breath was hot on her crown, his muscles hard where he gripped her, crowded her, getting off on having her at his mercy, thanks to the filled syringe of Death Stare, along with the snub-nosed pistol he'd made a show of safetying and sticking in his pocket, as if daring her to go for it.

They were alone in the lab trailer, just as she and Jack had been the day before, but that was where the similarities ended because the trailer was parked inside a huge city warehouse, and activity hummed just outside. She had glimpsed other vehicles from the encampment, along with additional lab space, production areas and more of the paramilitary militiamen, now with white-coated drug cookers in the mix.

And it was those glimpses, along with the fact that she knew the truth about the mayor now, that said no matter what he claimed, no matter what he'd told Jack, he couldn't afford to let either of them go.

The sick terror rose higher, making her shake as she sat there motionless at the console, refusing to unlock the machine, because she knew that once it was working again, she was dead. So she was stalling, giving Jack time to get there.

He would come, she knew. No matter how badly she'd hurt him back at the P.D., he would come for her. She only hoped he realized just how dangerous Proudfoot was with his back against the wall and his scheme coming apart around him. More, from what she'd overheard, she knew he wasn't even the boss of the outfit. There was a bigger, badder mastermind behind it all…yet Proudfoot was claiming he would let her go if Jack did what he said.

She had seen his eyes when he'd said it, though, knew it was a lie.

Don't trust him! she'd wanted to scream into the phone.

She hadn't dared, though, because two of the militiamen—dark-haired twentysomethings with matching haircuts and shark-dead eyes—had been hanging on to her at the time. So she'd stayed silent then, and now she kept telling herself that Jack knew his job, that he would find a way to bring backup and surround the warehouse before making a move, intending to catch the criminals in addition to rescuing her.

Part of her, though, feared that he wouldn't go that route—it was the part of her that knew that if the situation were reversed, she would do exactly as his captor demanded, hoping against hope that she'd be able to get him free uninjured. *Oh, Jack.*

"You've got ten seconds to get started," he said, pressing the needle into her skin hard enough to prick her. She felt a tingle and her heart stuttered in her chest. Gasping, she flinched back, in a move that earned her a dry, nasty chuckle.

"Didn't like that, did you? Or maybe you did like it. Is that it?" He came at her again, this time with his thumb on the plunger. "You want a taste of the action? Is that what it's going to take to get you going?"

She lurched off to the side of her chair as nausea churned and her head started to spin. Were the symptoms psychosomatic, or had some of the drug already entered her bloodstream?

Abruptly losing interest in the game, he lifted the syringe, pointing it upward as he grabbed her arm, yanked her upright and shoved her once more toward the console. "Unlock it. Now."

His voice was cold, his eyes hard, his skin slick with sweat even though it was chilly and damp inside the trailer. And she was running out of time. She had to think of something, a way to stall, a way to escape—but her thoughts kept scattering like starlings flushed from a New England oak, swerving and darting with rough, raucous screeches. "I can't," she whispered. "I need my laptop. It's back at the crime lab. It's got my—"

"Yo! Mr. Mayor!" a man's voice shouted from outside the trailer. "Got a visitor here."

Proudfoot's face split in a fierce, feral smile. He didn't take his eyes off her as he raised his voice to call, "Bring him in. I think our little amateur hacker here needs some encouragement."

"No," she whispered, understanding now why he'd wanted Jack there, too.

The same two toughs who'd helped the mayor earlier—she thought they might have been the men she and Jack had bumped into on their way out of the trailer before, looking for revenge now—came through the door hustling Jack between them at gunpoint. His hands were up, his holsters empty and his shirt torn, but his eyes went immediately to her, searching with silent rage and a secret agony that let her know that he'd been scared for her, that he cared, that he hadn't totally given up on her just yet.

And thank God for that.

"Tori," he said, voice breaking on her name.

"Shut it," one of the toughs said, jabbing him all the way into the trailer with the butt of his machine gun.

Proudfoot straightened away from her, attention fixed on Jack. To the men, he said, "Did you see anyone else?"

"Didn't even get a whiff. He's alone."

"Good. Keep him over there." Turning back to Tori, he said, "I don't for a second believe that you need your laptop, or any other damn thing except what's inside your head." He lifted the syringe and depressed the plunger until a bead of clear liquid ran from the tip. "Unlock the machine, or your boyfriend here gets the needle."

Steely-eyed, Jack met Tori's gaze. "Do it. Save yourself." But his urgent expression seemed to be telegraphing something else, and when he turned to snarl at one of his captors and then looked back at her, she saw his mouth move in a one-word command: *Stall.*

New energy coursed through her at the hint of a plan, of a possibility for rescue. She felt a flush stain her cheeks, but fought not to let anything else show.

"You heard him." Proudfoot spun back to her. "Get going."

Out of options and out of time, she turned slowly to the console. It would take only a couple of minutes for her to undo what she'd done to the programming, although the mayor wouldn't know that. So she started keying in commands, using as many steps as she could possibly come up with. As she worked, she glanced repeatedly at Jack, who glowered at his guards and pretended to ignore her. Each time she looked over, though, his fingers curled slightly, miming a caress.

The move warmed her, reassured her. Not just because of the intimacy that it implied, but also because she noticed it and understood it, just as she had caught his nearly invisible cue that she needed to stall. They were right back on the same page, working as the partners they had become up in the backcountry, though they were on his turf now, deep in the heart of the city.

They might have come back down to civilization and

the real-world problems it represented, but they hadn't totally left behind what they had found up in the mountains.

"Hey," Proudfoot said, catching her looking too long at Jack. "Knock it off and hurry the hell up! We haven't got all day."

Unfortunately, she didn't know how long they did have. What was Jack waiting for? Would she know it when it happened? And how much longer was it going to take? *Think,* she told herself. *Stall!* But she was almost done with the programming, didn't know how to stretch it out any longer without making it obvious.

The panic she'd held at bay since Jack's arrival threatened to overtake her once more, reminding her that she was powerless, useless, couldn't save herself never mind help him. Worse, what if they didn't get out of there? Her heart shuddered at the thought of never getting to apologize to him for wimping out back at the P.D. Because that was what she'd done.

"You can do this, Tori." His voice reached her, stroked along her skin like the caress of his hands had done the night before. "Go ahead. You can do it."

"She'd better do it," Proudfoot growled, "and soon."

Ignoring him, she stretched out her hand toward Jack, mouth working wordlessly for a moment before she got out, "I thought I'd never see you again." And though she might be stalling, it was the absolute truth. "I thought that it was over, that—"

"Don't," he interrupted, voice low. His eyes were locked on hers, clear and cerulean-blue, as if cleared now of all the doubts and regrets that had clouded them earlier. Her focus tunneled down to that sight, making it seem as if they were alone in the room when he continued, "We both made some wrong assumptions about some things, maybe some too-fast decisions about others. We can fix it, given time."

But time wasn't on their side, was it? More, she didn't need to wait, didn't want to wait. She wanted him to know what was in her heart here and now, without any strategy or plan, and without holding back the usual reserve that had protected her for so long…and in the process, she realized now, had hidden her away from things, too.

She had felt more in the past few days with him than she had in years of no harm, no foul encounters. And, granted, not everything she'd felt had been positive—he made her mad sometimes, made her crazy other times—but each of those feelings had been sharp and real, and they'd made her feel so damn alive she almost couldn't stand it. Even now, with Proudfoot looming over her, his patience running out, her blood buzzed from the almost-palpable connection she shared with the man who stood across the room from her at gunpoint, his eyes steady on hers.

I don't want to lose this, she realized. She didn't want to lose *him.* Her heart drummed against her ribs at the realization.

"Then we'll take whatever time we need to fix things," she said, and felt something unlock inside her as she made the decision. "We'll back up, take it slow, get to know each other. We'll do it your way, and I'll stick around for as long as it's working for both of us." Her lips trembled into a smile at his shock. "It'll be a different kind of adventure for me."

"No," he said, sounding shattered. "I don't—"

Without warning, gunfire split the air outside the trailer,

followed by the sound of running feet, shouted orders, cries of alarm.

"Tori, take cover!" Jack shouted and flung himself on his captors, somehow wrestling both of them to the ground simultaneously.

Heart lodged in her throat—both from the attack and from his "No, I don't…" because she didn't like the sound of that—she started for the kneehole of the nearest metal desk, but then swung around, screaming a "No!" of her own at the sight of Proudfoot heading for the fight with the syringe extended, going for Jack's broad-shouldered back. "Jack, look out!"

But he didn't hear her, or if he did, couldn't pull out of his struggle with the two burly guards in time to meet the new threat.

Tori didn't stop to think or plan. She just flung herself straight at Proudfoot, leaping on his back and taking him down flat on his face.

He landed with a crash and the .38 flung from his pocket and skidded under a DNA sequencer as he went limp. For a stunned second Tori sat there astride him with her knees stinging from the impact and her brain trying to catch up to the fact that she'd actually done it. She'd taken down the mayor!

The syringe, though. Where was the syringe? She had to get that away from him and neutralize the threat.

With her hands shaking, then her whole body starting to follow suit in reaction, she pushed off Proudfoot, who had fallen on his hands. Over near the door, Jack had one of the guards down and was squared off opposite the other. Outside, the gunfight continued unabated and a glance out the window didn't give her any clue whether the cops or militiamen were winning.

The syringe. Got to get the syringe. If it came down to it, she could take out Jack's remaining adversary with it.

Her heart drummed a sick rhythm at the thought, but she steeled herself and grabbed the mayor's shirt and waistband. Just as she started to roll him, Jack caught the second guard in the side of the head with a machine-gun stock, and the guy went down in a limp heap. Victory! She let go of Proudfoot and started to stand just as Jack straightened away and turned toward her, eyes fierce and alight.

Without warning, fiery pain erupted in her thigh, followed by a blur of motion as Proudfoot rose, brandishing the now-empty syringe.

She screamed and lurched back as Jack bellowed, "No!" and raced toward her, swinging the machine gun like it was a baseball bat and the mayor's head was the ball.

The impact made a hollow slapping sound and Proudfoot went down hard. Jack staggered a little as he turned and reached for her, then brought himself up short, eyes gone wide and anguished. "Hang on," he rasped, "I'll get you through the lines and out to a medic, I promise. They'll take care of you. They'll know what to do."

Already, though, she could feel the drug spreading and taking hold. She reached for him. "Jack." Dismay rocketed through her, along with despair and a burst of anger that she'd been given so little time with him. As he took the last two steps separating them, she swayed and crumpled to the ground, landing partly atop Proudfoot, who was well and truly unconscious this time, not just faking it.

Unfortunately, she was headed in the same direction

and she didn't know whether she'd be coming back from it. It seemed unbelievable to think this might be it, but she of all people knew they didn't have the antidote right yet. It hadn't been optimized, hadn't been tried on a cell system, never mind a patient.

And if this was it…

Grayness.

She came back around, panicked. "Jack!"

"I'm here." His voice was right in her ear, his cheek pressed to her temple. As those inputs became clear, she could also feel his arms around her and hear the quick thud of his heart beneath her face where it pressed on his chest. Or maybe that was her heart. She wasn't sure, couldn't separate one sensation from another through the spinning in her head and the fractured reality of the Death Stare high.

She knew one thing for certain, though, and it needed to be said now. So she forced herself all the way back to consciousness and opened her eyes through an effort of will.

When she saw mountain lakes, she smiled. "There you are."

Jack's skin was gray, his eyes stark, his voice broken as he rasped her name.

Lifting a hand to his cheek as she had done when they made love, she whispered, "For the record, I wouldn't have needed to take it slow. I already know that you're the one for me." She reached up and kissed him, and tasted tears. "I love you, Jack. And I'm so very sorry for leaving you like this."

His face crumpled; his eyes filled. And as the world grayed out, she heard him roar out her name and felt him scoop her up in his arms as if she weighed nothing. Which at that moment was exactly what she was feeling.

Nothing.

JACK MIGHT HAVE PULLED OFF walking through armed camps and police stations by marching along and making it look like he had someplace to be in a hurry, but kicking open the door of a drug trailer and stalking down from it carrying an unconscious woman in his arms wasn't exactly subtle.

He'd scouted first, though; all the guns that swung instantly to cover him belonged to the good guys.

"Hold!" Tucker's voice called the moment he cleared the door, followed by, "Stand down." And then the ranks broke and Tucker was headed for him, followed closely by several other cops, good men who he'd known most of his life. Tucker's face was creased with concern. "Was she shot?"

"Took a syringeful of the drug meant for me." And he suspected that fact would haunt him for the rest of his life, especially if she didn't pull through.

She was going to pull through, though. He intended to make sure of that.

Tucker blanched. "Damn, Jack."

"Don't," he said harshly, feeling himself start to crack under the threat of sympathy. "She's going to be fine." Jerking his head back toward the lab trailer. "You'll want cuffs and transpo for three guys. One of them's Proudfoot."

Tucker's expression flattened toward relief, but he said only, "Good work, Detective." Now wasn't the time for celebration.

Jack nodded. "Thanks for coming. Glad you got the message."

"Stealing my phone and Alyssa's car was a nice touch." Tucker held out Jack's cell, which still showed his text message of *He's got Tori. Find me when you get this.*

"Figured you could track one or the other of them." Jack shrugged, pulled Tucker's bells-and-whistles phone out of his pocket, and made the exchange. "I needed the head start and couldn't trust anyone else to make sure I got it."

"And you're way too used to going it alone. Maybe it's time you rethought that part of things and started letting someone else inside."

"I already did." Jerking his head in a nod, Jack turned and headed for the wide warehouse doorway, and the blinking lights of an ambulance beyond.

Someone had called for the paramedics, who came hustling in and tried to take Tori away, but he snarled them down and carried her out himself. He was peripherally aware of the task force members swarming the warehouse complex, and knots of militiamen seated in cuffs, leaning back-to-back under armed guard as they awaited buses to come and transport them to lockup.

"We did it, Ray," he murmured under his breath. "We broke the Death Stare case." But where only days earlier that one case had been the driving force in his universe, it far paled in significance compared to the woman who lay too cool and still in his arms, her body flowing like water, limp and unresisting as he lowered her to a proffered gurney. "I'm riding with her," he said flatly, "and we're leaving now."

He didn't think twice about abandoning the scene.

Tucker and the others were good cops, good men. They could handle things just fine without him. He, on the other hand, wasn't handling things nearly so well because as the ambulance accelerated away from the warehouse, blipping its sirens when necessary, he found himself leaning over Tori, counting her too-slow breaths and hoping she would open her eyes...yet at the same time glad she hadn't, because as long as she kept them closed she was still fighting the stare.

"Hang on, baby. Just hang on." He gripped her hands between his, squeezing tightly in hope that wherever she was inside, she could feel the pressure and knew he was there.

"Detective!" The paramedic looked aggrieved, like he'd been trying to get Jack's attention for some time.

"Sorry. What?"

"What more can you tell us about this drug? Is there a treatment yet? Anything?"

He shook his head. "I don't... Wait." Earlier, he'd been so irritated with her for the whole "Jack doesn't figure into this" line that he hadn't totally paid attention to the other things she and her tech had been talking about. He knew, though, that she had sent the information on the antidote off to her lab, to have them working on it in parallel with the feds. "Hang on."

Heart drumming with the sudden influx of potential hope, he dialed Information, rattled off the name of her university and department, and when he got an actual person, identified himself and said, "Put me through to Tori Bay's lab."

There was a pause and a couple of clicks, and then a distant phone started to ring. On the third digital burble, the line went live and a semi-familiar voice said, "Bay Laboratory."

"Is this Chondra?"

There was a pause, and then a cautious "Yes. Who is this?"

"This is Jack…hell, this is Tori's detective, and I need your help badly. What's more, *she* needs your help." He rattled off a quick summary of what had happened, steam-rolling over Chondra's gasps and exclamations. "I'm sorry to throw this on you all at once, but we really don't have time for you to be upset right now. I need to know if you've made any new progress on the antidote since you last talked to Tori."

Her eyes fired instantly. "Yes, I have. I coordinated with my friend who used to work in the Howard lab, and—"

"Hang on. I'm going to give you to the paramedic. Tell him anything he can do to help over the next ten minutes, and then brief him on whatever the doctor's going to need when we get to the hospital. You need stuff flown in, you tell him. I don't care if it's rare, expensive or exists solely on Mars, you tell us what she needs and I'll make sure she gets it." Or die trying. Because if she didn't make it… No, he wasn't going to think about that. Not when he intended to do anything and everything in his power to prevent it from happening.

"Okay, hand me over…and Jack?"

"Yeah."

"We're going to get her through this. I promise."

He handed over the phone without another word, not sure he could speak just then without breaking down. Because as he turned back to Tori, her words echoed in his soul. *I already know you're the one for me,* and *I love you.*

Yeah. He knew how both of those felt finally, after all this time. Tightening his grip on her hand, he bent over her, pressed his lips to her temple and whispered, "You're the one for me, too, Tori. I love you, and I'm not letting you go without a fight."

Chapter Sixteen

It took two days of dialysis and regular administrations of Chondra's antidote, but Tori finally woke up clearheaded and ravenous. To her surprise, Tucker was sitting at the foot of her bed.

She blinked at him, trying not to be disappointed that Jack hadn't been the one waiting. Vague memories surfaced of his having been there other times when she had surfaced briefly but not stayed awake. Or was that wishful thinking? She sifted through those memories and worked her way back, trying to remember through the drugged haze. What exactly had happened in that warehouse? Had she really told him she loved him and that she would stay in Bear Claw and try to make a go of a real relationship with him?

And if so, why wasn't he here?

Not letting herself panic quite yet, though the potential was definitely there, she focused on Tucker. In a voice gone husky with disuse, she said, "I'll owe you anything you want in exchange for a quart of Chunky Monkey."

His face creased into a smile. He looked far better-rested than he had the prior times their paths had crossed, making her think things were going okay for Bear Claw.

"I think we can arrange something, though no promises on the flavor."

She ended up with a cup of partway-melted chocolate ice cream that tasted like heaven. While she shoveled it inelegantly into her mouth, feeling like she was trying to catch up from two weeks of unconsciousness, not two days, Tucker brought her up to speed on the case.

"Let's see, what else? Proudfoot is in jail. He tried to cut a deal, but given the number of militiamen who had also been snagged in the warehouse raid, we've got plenty to go on when it comes to finding this Investor they were all working for. We don't have him yet, but it's only a matter of time. As for the Forgotten, your people and a couple of other groups got together and came up with a spray that kills off the fungus. It's not clear yet whether the infected trees will ever recover, but at least you guys managed to stop the spread before it hit Bear Claw Canyon." His voice softened. "You've got our gratitude for that one, Doc."

"Just doing my job," she said, then felt a twinge because that had been Jack's line.

Why was she thinking of him in the past tense? Why did it feel like she wasn't going to see him again?

Her stomach knotted on the thought that maybe she'd heard him say something—like "goodbye"—that she hadn't consciously registered at the time, but now her subconscious was trying to clue her in.

"Listen," she began, "can you tell me—"

"What we're doing to keep you safe, given that you not only know how to scramble the Investor's equipment, you could probably reproduce the fungus for him if coerced? You're going to have to go into protective custody for a bit, I'm afraid. Although in your case I don't think it'll feel all that different from what you're used to. You'll stay on the move, live out of a series of safe houses and keep working on the case remotely. Then, once the Investor is caught and the danger is over, you can go back to your life. Until he's out of the picture, you're not safe back at your university, and you're sure as hell not safe here in Bear Claw."

"Protective custody…" she said softly, not ready to believe it. And also aware that he'd deliberately misunderstood her question, and he hadn't once mentioned Jack. Disappointment shuddered through her and she pushed away the last of the ice cream. "When do I leave?"

"In a few hours, assuming all your tests come back okay." Tucker stood. "I'll be here to escort you to your transport. In the meantime, there'll be a uniformed officer outside your door at all times." He paused. "I'm serious, you know. This city owes you a huge debt…and because of what you've done for us, you're not going to be safe until the Investor is caught."

She nodded numbly. "Don't worry, I'll behave." She told herself not to ask, but couldn't not ask. "Where's Jack?"

Tucker's eyes slid away from hers. "He's been reassigned." He shrugged. "Sorry. Can I…ah, can I get you anything else before I go?"

Yes, she thought. *Absolutely. I want to see Jack.* She didn't say it, though, because he would have been there if he'd wanted to be, or else Tucker would have told her he was coming back. Because neither of those things had happened, the evidence suggested a single conclusion: he was bailing on her. Worse, he didn't even have the guts to do it in person. He was just planning on letting her be whisked off into protective custody without saying goodbye.

God, she had thought better of him.

"No," she said to Tucker. "I'm fine." She wasn't fine, not really, but she wasn't about to tell him that.

When he was gone, she was left alone in a private room that had more than its share of flowers and get-well cards, most from people she'd never met. And lying there, she tried to remember exactly what had happened between her and Jack in the warehouse, what they had each said. She could round up snippets but not whole conversations, which frustrated her, as did the doctors who came in and poked and prodded her, and the creeping fatigue that reminded her how badly out of whack the drug had thrown her body.

Finally, in the brief quiet following a reflex test, she closed her eyes to rest them for a moment. And fell dead asleep.

Her dreams were loud and Technicolor, and in them, she remembered telling Jack she loved him, and could swear she heard him whisper it back to her. So when she awoke to find him sitting at the foot of her bed, she smiled softly and her heart went *thudda-thudda* in her chest. "Hey," she said, "I missed you earlier."

"I had to take care of a few things."

He looked nervous, she realized, the dream warmth dissipating as disquiet took root. "What kind of things? And why didn't Tucker tell me where you were?"

"I asked him not to. I wanted to tell you myself." He rose and came to sit on the edge of the bed, and take her hands in his, expression solemn.

Her mouth dried to dust. "Tell me what?" She barely managed to get the words out.

"Remember how you said you'd stay in Bear Claw with me?"

Icy heat flashed through her, leaving her badly off balance. She couldn't speak, couldn't think, couldn't do much other than nod numbly. "You never answered me."

"I know." He paused. "You also said you loved me."

"Ditto." Her voice shook on the word. What was he getting at? "I do. I love you." She couldn't believe she was saying it, and that she had said it first. It was the truth, though. "I love you so much that the location doesn't matter. You matter. Giving things between us a chance matters."

"Good." He breathed out a long, slow sigh of relief. "It's damn good to hear you say that especially given that I just leased out my place and put most of my stuff in storage."

"Wait. What?" But even as she said the words, a starburst of hope started unfolding inside her. "You?" she asked, putting it together suddenly and getting a most glorious answer. "You're in charge of my protective custody? But that means…"

"Exactly." He brought their joined hands to his lips and pressed a kiss to her knuckles. And then, over her hand, he said, "Tori Bay, will you come away with me? Better yet, will you show me some of the places you love, and discover some new ones with me?"

She hadn't realized her heart had stopped beating for a moment, but it must have because suddenly it started up again, thudding to a newer, stronger beat. "But what about your job?" she protested. "What about your family?"

"Tucker says there'll always be a place for me in Bear Claw, especially now that the city is finally in line for a decent mayor. As for my family, they'll be here when we get back. And they'll be happy I took the time off so we could get to know each other and figure out if we're going to be family, too."

It wasn't a proposal, but it was close enough to have her lifting her free hand to her chest as her heart did a little dance. "Oh, Jack," she breathed. "Really? You'd leave it all behind for me?"

"I'll do whatever it takes to keep you safe, Tori. More important, I'll do whatever it takes to stay at your side. If that means we bounce around a bit, then we bounce around. If we agree to try putting down roots somewhere, then that's what we'll do. Right now, all I care is that we give this a chance."

"Oh, *Jack*."

He leaned over their hands, bent down and kissed her. What started out as a chaste brush of the lips caught fire almost immediately as she softened and yielded, and he groaned and took it deeper. Reaching up, she twined her arms around his neck and drew him down, until he was lying partway on top of her and their kiss turned real and searching. A groan reverberated in his chest and his hands went almost rough on her as he dragged caresses along her body and back up again.

She understood, though, because she felt it, too. "It's okay," she whispered to him, "I'm here. I'm fine. I'm not going anywhere without you."

Finally, he stilled, took a long and shuddering breath and levered himself off her to look down, smiling tenderly. "Is that a yes? You'll give us a chance?"

"I don't need to give us a chance—I already know that I love you, even though it's not our fifth date."

"Tenth," he corrected. "And I love you, too." Then he stood and held out his hand. "Are you ready to go? The doctors have cleared you and there's a plane waiting for us at the airport."

And although that was normally one of her favorite things to hear —that it was time to visit a new place, start a new adventure—now she found herself hesitating.

"What's wrong?"

She had to laugh at herself. "I'm just realizing how much I'm going to miss Bear Claw and the Forgotten." She slanted him a look. "We'll have to come back as soon as it's safe, you know."

If she hadn't been looking for it, she might not have noticed his soft exhale or the slight shift of his weight that said he was relieved. She noticed those things, though, and it warmed her to know that she could give him that sense of relief, and that it was as precious to her as her own anticipation of a new adventure.

He seemed to see that because his fingers tightened on hers and his lake-blue eyes filled with love. "We're going to be okay, aren't we?"

She smiled up at him. "Something tells me we're going to be better than okay." Because while they might not have been perfect, they were exactly perfect for each other.

* * * * *

SUSPENSE

Heartstopping stories of intrigue and mystery—
where true love always triumphs.

Harlequin
INTRIGUE

COMING NEXT MONTH
AVAILABLE JANUARY 10, 2012

#1323 CERTIFIED COWBOY
Bucking Bronc Lodge
Rita Herron

#1324 NATE
The Lawmen of Silver Creek Ranch
Delores Fossen

#1325 COWBOY CONSPIRACY
Sons of Troy Ledger
Joanna Wayne

#1326 GREEN BERET BODYGUARD
Brothers in Arms
Carol Ericson

#1327 SUDDEN INSIGHT
Mindbenders
Rebecca York

#1328 LAST SPY STANDING
Thriller
Dana Marton

You can find more information on upcoming Harlequin® titles,
free excerpts and more at www.HarlequinInsideRomance.com.

HICNM1211

REQUEST YOUR FREE BOOKS!
2 FREE NOVELS PLUS 2 FREE GIFTS!

Harlequin

INTRIGUE

BREATHTAKING ROMANTIC SUSPENSE

YES! Please send me 2 FREE Harlequin Intrigue® novels and my 2 FREE gifts (gifts are worth about $10). After receiving them, if I don't wish to receive any more books, I can return the shipping statement marked "cancel." If I don't cancel, I will receive 6 brand-new novels every month and be billed just $4.49 per book in the U.S. or $5.24 per book in Canada. That's a saving of at least 14% off the cover price! It's quite a bargain! Shipping and handling is just 50¢ per book in the U.S. and 75¢ per book in Canada.* I understand that accepting the 2 free books and gifts places me under no obligation to buy anything. I can always return a shipment and cancel at any time. Even if I never buy another book, the two free books and gifts are mine to keep forever.

182/382 HDN FEQ2

Name _____ (PLEASE PRINT)

Address _____ Apt. #

City _____ State/Prov. _____ Zip/Postal Code

Signature (if under 18, a parent or guardian must sign)

Mail to the Reader Service:
IN U.S.A.: P.O. Box 1867, Buffalo, NY 14240-1867
IN CANADA: P.O. Box 609, Fort Erie, Ontario L2A 5X3

Not valid for current subscribers to Harlequin Intrigue books.

**Are you a subscriber to Harlequin Intrigue books
and want to receive the larger-print edition?
Call 1-800-873-8635 or visit www.ReaderService.com.**

* Terms and prices subject to change without notice. Prices do not include applicable taxes. Sales tax applicable in N.Y. Canadian residents will be charged applicable taxes. Offer not valid in Quebec. This offer is limited to one order per household. All orders subject to credit approval. Credit or debit balances in a customer's account(s) may be offset by any other outstanding balance owed by or to the customer. Please allow 4 to 6 weeks for delivery. Offer available while quantities last.

Your Privacy—The Reader Service is committed to protecting your privacy. Our Privacy Policy is available online at www.ReaderService.com or upon request from the Reader Service.

We make a portion of our mailing list available to reputable third parties that offer products we believe may interest you. If you prefer that we not exchange your name with third parties, or if you wish to clarify or modify your communication preferences, please visit us at www.ReaderService.com/consumerschoice or write to us at Reader Service Preference Service, P.O. Box 9062, Buffalo, NY 14269. Include your complete name and address.

HI11B

*Brittany Grayson survived a horrible ordeal at the hands
of a serial killer known as The Professional…
who's after her now?*

*Harlequin® Romantic Suspense presents a new installment
in Carla Cassidy's reader-favorite miniseries,*
LAWMEN OF BLACK ROCK.

Enjoy a sneak peek of
TOOL BELT DEFENDER.

*Available January 2012
from Harlequin® Romantic Suspense.*

"**B**rittany?" His voice was deep and pleasant and made
her realize she'd been staring at him openmouthed through
the screen door.

"Yes, I'm Brittany and you must be…" Her mind suddenly went blank.

"Alex. Alex Crawford, Chad's friend. You called him
about a deck?"

As she unlocked the screen, she realized she wasn't
quite ready yet to allow a stranger inside, especially a male
stranger.

"Yes, I did. It's nice to meet you, Alex. Let's walk around
back and I'll show you what I have in mind," she said. She
frowned as she realized there was no car in her driveway.
"Did you walk here?" she asked.

His eyes were a warm blue that stood out against his
tanned face and was complemented by his slightly shaggy
dark hair. "I live three doors up." He pointed up the street to
the Walker home that had been on the market for a while.

"How long have you lived there?"

"I moved in about six weeks ago," he replied as they

walked around the side of the house.

That explained why she didn't know the Walkers had moved out and Mr. Hard Body had moved in. Six weeks ago she'd still been living at her brother Benjamin's house trying to heal from the trauma she'd lived through.

As they reached the backyard she motioned toward the broken brick patio just outside the back door. "What I'd like is a wooden deck big enough to hold a barbecue pit and an umbrella table and, of course, lots of people."

He nodded and pulled a tape measure from his tool belt. "An outdoor entertainment area," he said.

"Exactly," she replied and watched as he began to walk the site. The last thing Brittany had wanted to think about over the past eight months of her life was men. But looking at Alex Crawford definitely gave her a slight flutter of pure feminine pleasure.

Will Brittany be able to heal in the arms of Alex,
her hotter-than-sin handyman...or will a second
psychopath silence her forever? Find out in
TOOL BELT DEFENDER
Available January 2012
from Harlequin® Romantic Suspense
wherever books are sold.